THE GOLDEN MOUNTAIN:

a Complete Tale of the Seven Dwarves

Elizabeth Gallegos

I want to thank my amazing friends and family for their encouragement and help with editing. I appreciate all your patience and kind words! Amanda, you were terrific, keeping me going when I thought I should stop. Dad, I loved every day we worked together, finding humor every step of the way.

CONTENTS

THE GOLDEN MOUNTAIN:

A complete tale of The Seven Dwarves

By: Elizabeth Gallegos

CH. 1   FIRST DRINK, FIRST LOVE

The night was warm as a gentle summer breeze lazily crawled across the town. Despite the evening breeze, the summer heat remained pervasive. There was just no relief from the heatwave. Laus was a modest town of dwarves, and the homes reflected that uncomplicated lifestyle.

In the home of the Greybear family, tears were shedding for the matron, Winnie. She had drawn her last breath as she pushed her first and only child into the world. Angelo squeezed his wife's warm lifeless hand in anguish. The cries of his newborn son couldn't break past the pain of the crushing loss of his Winnie.

The bedroom door flung open as the midwife rushed in. Her chest was heaving as she desperately tried to catch her breath. Having come from delivering another child, she had to run the entire way to the Greybear house only to discover she was too late. As she approached the bedside, Angelo started to wail. His cheeks were shiny and wet from the rivers of tears that were flowing from his eyes. The pain of losing her was unbearable and overwhelmed him.

Seeing the newborn babe, unclean and lying beside his mother, the midwife reached out to the child. Angelo thought she was reaching out to console him. He flailed his arms at her, not wanting her pity.

"You are too late!" His words were choked out and soaked in great anger and deep anguish. He grabbed her arm tightly and pulled her towards the front door.

"Wait!" she gasped. "The babe!" Still trying to aid the newborn child, the midwife was pushed out of the house and into the street. Angelo firmly shut the front door and latched it.

Angelo returned to his wife's bedside, finally hearing the cries of the newborn babe. Looking at his son for what felt like the first time, Angelo's joy as a new father was washed away by his grief and anger.

Winnie had been so excited and had planned to name the babe Trussi if it was a boy. Even this memory brought Angelo no comfort. Angelo grabbed a long decorated cloth Winnie had proudly made months earlier. Wrapping the baby absentmindedly, he sat down beside the bed and wept.

Angelo sat there angry, scared, and alone. He felt empty without Winnie, as she was everything to him. Even holding Trussi brought him no comfort. Her loss was more than he could bear.

17 Years Later

The summer sun was bright and hot, but the breeze finally cooled off. Trussi worked in the fields like so many of the townsfolk. They needed to work quickly now as the harvest was near. This year, the town's crops flourished and were bountiful. Which meant there was more work to be completed. Trussi was a hard worker and was considered quite strong among the other dwarves. He worked more hours than the others and always did so without complaint. Even in the summer midday heat, he could work steadily without losing his pace.

At the end of this day's work, Trussi headed home. He was a quiet person and would often avoid socializing with others. He rarely knew what topics to discuss. He also found conversation with others rather dull and often meaningless. His home was on the opposite end of town from the fieldwork. He had to walk past many houses and the village market while heading home. Within the market, few stands remained open this late in the day. Trussi stopped by one of the still-open vendors he knew well and picked up ample food for the evening before continuing home.

Before arriving at his own home, Trussi made a minor detour to a homely-looking house. Inside this house, he knew three children and their widowed mother. Her husband had been sick with a fever and passed away not long ago, leaving the remaining family in hardship.

Trussi placed some food he had just purchased by their front door. He knocked firmly and then walked away. If he had stayed, it would have meant having one of those conversations he avoided, even if it was only an expression of gratitude. He continued home with his pace unhurried. The long walk was quite comforting and relaxing to him. It was his 'special' time that he genuinely enjoyed.

As he arrived at his home, Trussi paused momentarily and then entered. The house was small but comfortable and was built originally by his grandmother. Angelo had moved in shortly after Trussi was born, probably saving his life as an infant. Trussi's grandmother had raised him and taught him most of what he learned to this day. Despite his father's constant presence, Trussi learned nothing from him beyond his ugliness of wallowing in sorrow and self-pity.

The central room had a hearth with a few old utensils. Trussi knew how to use them all due to his grandmother's patient teachings. He first made the fire, and after Trussi filled the pot with everything for the stew, he gathered wild herbs and spices from behind his house on the hillside. Once he added the herbs, Trussi looked at the contents, satisfied with what he saw. It wasn't much, but it smelled wonderful and would fill his belly.

The stew was ready momentarily, and he poured the contents into two bowls. Trussi took one bowl to his father, who sat quietly and alone in his room. Angelo was scarcely the man he used to be, never leaving his room or talking with anyone. He ate less and less over time and had not eaten at all in the last few days. Trussi thought his father looked more like a skeleton than a man.

Trussi placed the bowl before his father, but Angelo didn't move. "Eat," Trussi said to him, indicating to partake of the fresh meal. Angelo's eyes shifted slowly to look at the bowl before him, but he still didn't move. Trussi left Angelo alone in the room with the hot food. He had done his part. It was not up to him whether or not his father ate.

Trussi returned to his bowl of stew by the hearth and ate slowly. He savored each bite of the only meal for that day. After he finished eating, Trussi sat by the fire. He began reading from the only book he owned. "The Golden Mountain" was its title. This book was the same one from which his grandmother had taught him how to read. Trussi had read it so many times that the pages were worn, and the cover crumbled at the edges.

Memories of his grandmother drifted into his thoughts as he held that old book. She had taught him nearly everything he knew, how to cook, what herbs to look for and where, and other survival skills. Two winters ago, Trussi had found her dead in her bed in the late morning as he went to check on her. She had passed away in her sleep during the night. She had not been sick but had been frail in her old age.

Trussi didn't realize how much he would miss her company until she was gone. He thought of her often, especially when he was feeling lonely. His father was of no comfort, and he had no other family or friends with whom to spend time.

Pushing down deep his feelings of solitude, Trussi started reading once again. He engulfed himself in the beloved tales of adventure and treasure within the aging pages. He read late until his eyes drooped, and sleep finally overtook him. Trussi dreamed he was the man in the story going on those glorious adventures to the golden mountain he had read about so many times. The treasures he found there made him laugh with joy!

Trussi jerked awake suddenly in the night. He was not sure if his dream had caused him to awaken or if it was something else. Confusion soon cleared away as he remembered falling asleep by the hearth while reading. It was dark since the fire was out, and all about him was quiet.

"Father?" Trussi called out, but no answer came.

Not that his father would ever respond to him anyway. Trussi got up, then dusted his pants off. Carefully, he placed his book in its proper spot. After stretching his stiff muscles, he slowly walked to his father's room. He would need to get Angelo into bed before returning to sleep.

Trussi entered his father's room. It was dark, but the moonlight from the open window was radiant enough to see everything within the room. The bowl of stew remained untouched, and his father was still sitting in his chair, slightly slumped over. He must have fallen asleep while sitting there.

"Come, father, let's get you to bed," Trussi told him. Angelo did not stir.

Trussi reached out to help his father, but he knew something was wrong immediately when he touched him. Angelo was cold to the touch and stiff. Trussi knew what that meant. It was the same as when he found his grandmother when she passed away. "F-father?!....no..." Trussi's words were quiet and barely left his lips.

He tried to shake his father's shoulder as if that might wake him. But his father remained cold and motionless. No stirring or fluttering of his eyes or breath passed his lips. Angelo, Trussi's father, was dead.

He expected to feel grief or sadness. Instead, all he felt was anger. His fists clenched as his arms rose quickly, nearly hitting the wall. The muscles in his hands and arms were so tight they began to shake and ache. Trussi slowly lowered his arms and concentrated on reducing his rapid breathing, calmly taking his breaths slower.

After what seemed like an eternity, his fists and anger slowly relaxed. Once Trussi had composed himself, he thought about summoning a doctor. However, he realized that retrieving a doctor would be pointless. His father was gone, and no doctor could bring him back. There were no family members or friends to contact about his passing. All that was left to do was for

Trussi to bury his father.

Trussi was tired but knew that he needed to finish it tonight. He had to work in the morning as considerable harvesting was still left. Despite the darkness outside, Trussi located the shovel and pickaxe from the back of the house. He removed his shirt and started digging his father's grave. Trussi decided it would be next to his grandmother's grave as he decided she deserved some company in death.

He used the shovel for the softer top earth and the pickaxe for the deeper ground, which was firmer and denser with rocks. As he dug deeper, Trussi used his anguished thoughts of anger to fuel each pickaxe swing. It was a slight release, and his anger slowly diminished as his task neared completion.

Sweat dripped down his face, chest, and back. His lungs began to burn as he pressed through the hard work. His arms vibrated with the numbness that came from complete exhaustion. He dropped the tool next to the deep hole he had just dug. Trussi had completed his father's grave.

After walking to his father's room, Trussi noticed the body was stiff from rigor setting in. With the body's odd position, dragging him to the grave would not be possible. Trussi took a deep breath and scooped his father up in his arms. His father was barely more than a skeleton now and lighter to carry than he expected.

He carried the body to the new grave at the back of the house. Dropping it in carelessly, Trussi stood there, unsure if he should say any words out of respect for the dead. 'Screw it!' he thought. His father had given up on life, and any respect Trussi had for him was long gone. Using the shovel, he filled the grave and put the tools away.

Trussi was sweaty, stinky, and covered in filth. He wanted to go inside and pass out from exhaustion, but his grandmother's words about cleanliness echoed in his head. So, instead of returning to the house, he headed further past the small pasture beside the home.

A creek was nearby, and the moonlight was bright enough that he could see his way there without any trouble. The water was cool and refreshing. It wasn't deep enough to swim in, but deep enough so that as he bent down, he was completely submerged. After a few minutes of scrubbing himself clean, Trussi walked back home. The summer night was warm, and he was dry enough when he returned. Instead of returning to the hearth, he went to his father's room. 'Tonight,' he thought, 'I am going to sleep in a bed.'

He entered his father's room. 'No! This room is no longer my father's. It is mine.' Trussi thought to himself. He saw the cold bowl of uneaten stew and grabbed it without hesitation. Trussi felt famished after the work it took to bury his father. He placed the edge of the bowl to his lips and devoured its contents swiftly. Once done, he set the bowl down, and Trussi flopped onto the empty bed. Trussi instantly fell into a deep and dreamless sleep.

Sounds of a rooster crowing nearby woke Trussi. The sun had barely broken past the horizon, and streaks of sunlight danced around the room. It was time for him to get up. His muscles protested with immense soreness as he turned to get out of bed. Despite the pain, he got up. After taking a few steps, he stretched out his sorest muscles, which gave him some relief. Work waited for no one, and Trussi was needed in the harvesting fields today. He arrived in the fields just as everyone else appeared. He worked alongside everyone else, and although Trussi was slower than usual, he kept pace with the rest of the workers. Despite his soreness, today, he felt lighter somehow. It was as if he had a weight had lifted off of him. This feeling was weird and new, and he wasn't sure what to make of it.

Despite the hard work, Trussi noticed other workers speaking to each other in idle conversation. They even included speaking to him while discussing the weather, the crops, and a recent wedding. It felt nice to be included in each of the conversations, finally. This feeling was surprising to Trussi. He pondered why he had yet to speak much with others.

At the end of the workday, the group dispersed. As Trussi was leaving, he noticed some men, most of them unmarried, seemed cheerful as they discussed going to the local pub. To his surprise, one of the men invited Trussi to join them. He had never been there but knew what food and drink they served. Initially, he was hesitant but accepted the invitation as it was far more appealing than the prospect of going home to an empty house.

The group walked together to the pub, and some men bragged and made jokes along the way. Trussi did not know any of these humorous jokes and stories. However, he still enjoyed listening to them. He even chuckled along when an unexpected punchline surprised him. Once they reached the pub, they all went in together. The room inside was brightly lit and smelled of sweaty men, drink, and food. Patrons were laughing or arguing throughout the establishment. Others he noticed were describing tall tales of exaggerated strength or heroism. He liked it all instantly.

They were seated at a corner table and ordered a round of fermented cider. Trussi had never had alcohol himself but had observed others before who had drank, sometimes to excess. While they waited for their drinks, the others in the group continued telling jokes or started in on some exaggerated tale of their own.

While the others joked and laughed, Trussi had noticed one of the girls serving drinks at another table. She was young like him and had light brown wavy hair with freckles along her cheeks. He didn't remember seeing her before around the village, but maybe he had never noticed her. No, he decided. He would surely recognize her. She was far too pretty to forget. The guy sitting beside him suddenly slapped him on the back, bringing Trussi out of his trance.

"Admiring the local scenery, eh?" the man chuckled.

Trussi blushed a bit then. He didn't realize he had been noticeably staring at the poor girl. Just as he thought this, the waitress brought them their drinks. Trussi smiled as she placed a tall glass in front of him. She was slightly older and rounder than the other girl. But, even so, she was still lovely looking. The group cheered and expressed thanks, and the barmaid happily trotted away.

Without hesitation, the group began guzzling their drinks. Trussi looked down at his drink, then looked up to see the other girl again. Only, she was no longer there. Not paying much attention, he started taking a sip of his drink. The fermented cider was warm, and the alcohol within it tasted terrible. He unexpectedly half swallowed and half inhaled the first sip of his drink, then instantly started choking.

The man next to him slapped him on the back again. He laughed and asked, "Don't tell me this is your first drink?"

Trussi nodded, still coughing remnants of the cider out of his throat. The group around him roared with laughter, filling him with embarrassment.

"I've been coming here since I was 15!" one of the men boasted. The others raised their glasses at this comment making similar comments as well. The man next to him looked back at Trussi, grinning widely. "Don't worry! The more you drink, the better it gets!"

Trussi doubted that very much. In his experience, anything that tasted terrible never got better the more he had of it. Still, everyone else was drinking. They appeared to be enjoying themselves well enough. He took another drink and was careful not to choke on it.

"That's it!!" A member of his group shouted. Another round of laughing and cheering went around the table, and Trussi couldn't help but smile. No, he wasn't smiling. He was grinning! He took another big drink, this time not holding back. It still tasted terrible. Several more swigs followed, with each one going down easier. Trussi noticed the inside of his belly was starting to feel warm, and at the same time, the back of his head was feeling mildly tingly. It was a delightful and odd sensation. He discovered that he couldn't help but laugh with the others, finding humor in nearly everything said.

It wasn't long before he reached the bottom of his glass. Suddenly, the girl placed another full glass of fermented cider before him. Trussi looked up to thank her but was left open-mouthed when he saw the wavy brown-haired girl. She smiled and winked at him, then walked away, continuing to bring drinks and various food items to the other tables. His heart fluttered at the mere sight of her. Or perhaps it was the drink? Nothing felt like it did before. It was as if his head wasn't working correctly. Yes, he decided, it was most certainly the drink that made his chest feel fluttery. Or was it his stomach that felt fluttery?

Deciding he needed to leave immediately, Trussi guzzled down part of his new drink as fast as possible. He got up from the table and fabricated a polite excuse to leave. He paid his tab and exited the pub quickly. As he was walking, Trussi discovered the world had become wobbly. His initial steps caused him to stumble, though he slowly improved his footing as he went home.

Trussi reached his front door and entered without hesitation. He didn't stop to make a fire at the hearth like usual. Instead, he went straight to his new room and right to bed. Plopping down on the bed, he expected to fall asleep fast. Instead, Trussi lay there for a while. Images of the girl with the wavy-brown hair filled his groggy thoughts. He had never been interested in any girl before, and the sudden realization that he wanted to see her again filled him with dread. So much had changed in just one day. Sleep eventually came and carried him away from those thoughts. His dreams carried him far away and overflowed with adventure and treasure. And love. Yes, love.

CH. 2   A MAN AND A PLAN

Trussi woke up in the morning and found he was immensely thirsty. Once up, he went to the well in his backyard and couldn't raise the pail fast enough. He drank the cold water until he couldn't swallow anymore. His stomach didn't feel right, and his head was slightly groggy from the night. Despite this, he knew he still needed to work in the fields today. Trussi, still dressed in yesterday's clothes, decided that what he had on would suffice, and he left home for the fieldwork.

Walking to the fields, he felt unbelievably awful, but Trussi was determined to make it there regardless. Step by step, he eventually arrived at work. Trussi wasn't the first one there but was grateful not to be the last to arrive. The morning weather was already hot, and his pace started slower than usual. As midday approached, his groggy feeling waned. He was finally able to focus on his work and catch up with the fastest of the group.

At the end of the workday, the guys invited Trussi to join them at the Pub again. He had no intention of feeling this horrible ever again. As such, he politely turned down the invitation. Walking home, as usual, Trussi started thinking about the pretty girl he had seen at the Pub. Her wavy brown hair and the freckles on her cheeks began to fill his thoughts.

'No!' he thought angrily to himself. He needed to be thinking about practical things. Yet, Trussi couldn't get her out of his head. He stopped dead in his tracks. If he went to the Pub, he could see her again. 'No,' he thought again and again. He was going home! Trussi shook his head and continued on his way.

Then he thought about the way the girl had winked at him with a smile on her lips. Trussi stopped again and sighed. 'I better not regret this,' he thought as he smiled while changing his mind and turning around. Starting towards the Pub, a large grin formed, and his pace quickened.

Arriving shortly, Trussi hesitated just before entering. 'What am I doing?' he thought, almost panicked. Running his hands through his hair, he could already feel his heart pounding in his chest. 'Crap!' He thought about his situation but discovered he still wanted to see her again. 'I'm in trouble.'

Trussi considered turning around again and leaving, but that moment was fleeting. 'I am not a coward,' he encouraged himself and pushed the door open. Upon entering the Pub, he glanced around and found a small empty table. The moment he sat down, he began looking for the wavy-brown-haired girl. She was there, serving tables not far from him. Upon seeing her, Trussi's heart fluttered just as it had before. This time, he couldn't blame these feelings on the effect of the drink.

It was only a short time until she noticed him and approached his table. "Well, well!" She said and smiled at him. "All by yourself tonight?" Her eyes were the same golden brown that matched her wavy hair. "What will it be tonight, sir? Fermented cider?"

Trussi had no desire for any more fermented cider. "No, no thanks. Do you have any stew ready?" He tried to look away but discovered he couldn't take his eyes off her cute smile.

She shook her head, "I'm sorry. We ran out a short while ago. But there's fresh bread, plenty of porridge, and we always have boiled eggs. Can I get you some of that instead?"

"I'll take four boiled eggs and some bread, please."

She placed a hand on her hip and leaned forward. "Anything to drink?" she asked with a pleasant but expectant look.

She was so close to him that he could smell her fragrance. It was a mixture of apple cider and earthiness. "Just some water, please," he answered with a smile. The words came out hoarse but clear. The girl smiled brighter then and nodded as she left the table.

Not sure what to do next, Trussi let out a sigh. He wanted to talk with her more and more. He needed to get to know her and perhaps even learn her name. He looked around the Pub. Sadly, nearly every table was full. She would be far too busy for idle chat. It wasn't long before she returned, bringing the food and setting down a tall glass of water.

"Thank you, miss." He said as she placed his food plate on the table. Trussi then carefully placed his hand gently on top of hers. "Please, miss, might I ask you your name?"

The young barmaid lightly blushed. She pulled back her hand, and Trussi feared she would leave and complain about him. Instead, he heard her saying "Giada." She then blushed deeper and turned quickly to tend to the other tables.

'Giada!' Trussi thought with a growing longing. At last, he had a pretty name to go with that beautiful face! 'And it fits her perfectly!' he thought as he drank the cold water she had served him with those sweet, soft hands. He wanted to talk to her more, to learn everything he could about her. His heart was now pounding hard in his chest.

He hoped Giada would return and talk to him more, so Trussi ate his food very slowly. He drank his refreshing water unusually quickly. He had not yet fully recovered from the intense thirst he had felt all day. Giada came by with a pitcher, filling his empty cup. He smiled at her in thanks, and she winked back at him. He watched patiently as the other customers ate, drank, and eventually left. When a table cleared, Trussi was sure to finish his glass of water, and Giada wasn't far behind to fill it again. After drinking multiple cups of water, it didn't take long before he realized he needed to relieve himself.

When Giada returned to fill his glass again, he asked her where the lavatory was. She pointed to the hall entrance. "To the left."

As he rose, she placed her hand on his. "You can't use it until you pay your tab." His questioning eyes met hers, and she blushed just then.

"Sorry, house rules. Too many customers try to sneak out without paying."

"I understand. That's not a problem." Her hand was still on his. She leaned back as if she was going to walk away. Trussi twisted his hand quickly, clasping her hand in his. Without hesitation, he lifted her hand, bringing it to his lips, and lightly placed a kiss.

Giada gasped in surprise but smiled and blushed. She turned away slowly, returning to her other tables and the drinks she was serving. Trussi then paid his tab and left a small tip as well, and even though he knew where the lavatory was, he asked the bartender where it was anyway. It was good that he asked, as he needed a key to enter. He hurried to empty his bladder, which felt like it would burst any minute. He hadn't drunk any alcohol, and yet his head was still swimming, and his heart fluttering. 'I kissed her! I KISSED HER!! Well, I kissed her hand. That counts.' he thought with a telling smile.

As he left the lavatory, the bartender approached him and informed him they were closing the Pub. Trussi glanced around to see if he could find Giada and say good night, but she was no longer there. He nodded, thanked the man, and left. The walk home passed quickly, and his steps felt lighter. It didn't take much time for him to decide to return to the Pub tomorrow. He thought to himself that he might even go every night! After reaching his house, he went straight to bed. Lying there, Trussi could only think of Giada. 'This is it!' he thought. 'She is the one meant for me. The only one.' And with that final thought, he fell fast asleep with a smile still adorning his face.

As the days passed, Trussi visited the Pub each night after working in the fields. He always sat alone and ordered his food only from Giada. Every night was similar but different in his thoughts. His drink of choice remained water as the fermented cider had little appeal to him. Each day he thought of what he wanted to ask her so he could learn more about her. As Giada refilled his empty water glass, he would ask her questions each night. Such questions as what her favorite color was, her favorite flower, food, etc.

It didn't take Giada long to notice Trussi constantly asking her little questions. After several days she started to give additional tidbits of information about herself as she refilled Trussi's cup. She even began asking questions about him as well. After several weeks of this little banter repeating, Trussi was ready for more. He knew what he wanted, so he readied to court her. Returning to the Pub like normal, Trussi sat at a small table by himself and placed his usual order from Giada once she approached.

The night seemed to pass like usual. Giada returned to his table, refilling his glass of water. She would give small details about herself or ask something about him. As the night would become late and patrons started returning to their homes, Trussi knew it was time. He was so nervous he could feel his hands sweating. As Giada returned to his table to refill his water glass again, Trussi wiped his hands on his napkin. When Giada finished filling his glass, Trussi decided, 'This is it, now or never!' He reached up and lightly clasped her hand.

"Giada," his voice came out in a squeak, his nerves getting the best of him. He cleared his throat and tried again. "Giada, I have an important question to ask you." Giada's eyebrows raised as her eyes locked onto his. She nodded as an indication for him to proceed. He took a deep breath. "I was wondering, that is, I would like to ask your father's permission to court you." He was breathing hard as his heart hammered in his chest. It felt as if the world had stopped, waiting for her reply.

Her eyebrows furrowed, and she looked down towards her feet. "I don't know, Trussi." His heart sank. She didn't want him. His entire world was crashing down around him. Seeing his worried look, Giada clasped his hand tighter. "Oh, it's not that! I want you to court me!"

Trussi felt like his body would explode. She wanted him! Giada continued, "My father has always denied anyone who has asked to court me. He owns this Pub and says he wants me well cared for and supported. No one has been worthy enough to court me in his mind." She said this with a sad demeanor.

Trussi sighed. That was a problem he didn't expect. Giada perked up just then. "I have an idea! The blacksmith just lost his apprentice to a fever. I heard he is looking for a new apprentice but is having difficulty finding one. If you could become his apprentice, you would have an honorable trade. I am sure my father would consider you then."

Trussi wanted to be sure he understood what she meant. "If I become the blacksmith's apprentice, you think your father would allow a courtship with you?"

Giada nodded as an enormous grin covered her face, highlighting her cute dimples. "I'm sure of it!" Trussi stood up and couldn't help but grin as well.

"Then that's what I'll do. Whatever it takes." He kissed the back of her hand as she smiled. Giada blushed deeply. Trussi was entranced by her beauty once again.

"I...I have to get back to the rest of my patrons." Trussi nodded and released her hand. She winked at him before returning to serving her other tables.

He headed home, a new plan formulated in his head. Trussi had never considered becoming a blacksmith before. His entire family, grandparents, and great-grandparents had all worked in the fields. 'Becoming the blacksmith's apprentice! If that's what I need to do so I can court Giada, then that's what I'll do!' he thought with a smile. Newfound determination began to fill Trussi as he hurried home. He knew where the blacksmith's shop was and would be there early in the morning.

As he lay in bed that night, Trussi released a big sigh. Giada wanted him to court her, which meant she wanted to be with him as much as he wanted to be with her. Giada once again filled his dreams.

Trussi realized it was Sunday morning as he heard the church bells ringing in the distance. He sighed, wanting to shout out his frustration. There would be no working in the fields today. There would also be no one working in any of the shops. Everyone in town was devout in their faith and would be sure to attend church.

Trussi pulled up a pail of water from the well behind his house and cleaned up as quickly as possible. Once he changed into his Sunday best, he left for church. His impatience to speak with the blacksmith caused him to become irritated. Even though he usually enjoyed attending church, he wished today wasn't Sunday. The walk started slowly, but as his irritation boiled out, he stomped his legs with each step.

Suddenly, he thought of the possibility of seeing the blacksmith at church. After the service, most townsfolk stayed for several hours talking and being social with each other. Though he had never lingered for this before, he thought, 'perhaps I can find the blacksmith there and talk to him about becoming his apprentice! Yes!' Trussi's steps were now lighter, his frustration replaced with new anticipation.

Walking there was a bit of a trip. The church was built on the edge of town and atop the tallest hill. Since it was the highest point within the village, the added benefit of the location was that the bells could be heard easily by all in town each Sunday morning.

Once Trussi reached the church, he could hear the peaceful sounds of the choir singing from within. Going inside, he took a seat in the back. Once everyone was seated, the preacher stood up and began his prayers. During church, it usually felt peaceful to Trussi. But today, he found it immensely stressful. He had to talk to the blacksmith today. He just had to!

After what seemed like an eternity but was about an hour, they finally lined up for the tithing. Each person would get in line, whether man, woman, or child, and approach the basket before the preacher. They would then place their money or valuables in the basket. The preacher would then make a holy symbol in the air while praying and touching the person on the forehead with a blessing. The more someone tithed, the longer the prayer and blessings that person would receive.

Trussi waited in line, trying not to be impatient. 'This is going to drag on forever!' he impatiently thought. Once he finally reached the front of the line, he placed his usual tithing in the basket and received his accustomed prayer and blessing.

'Finally!' he thought. 'I can find the blacksmith.' Entering the gathering area, Trussi looked around for the blacksmith. People were talking in small clusters, so he started on one side and worked his way through.

He eventually found the blacksmith, who appeared to be talking with the local baker and doctor. They seemed relaxed in their discussion, and Trussi hoped he would be welcome to join the conversation. Walking towards them, Trussi thought about what he might say and how he might say it. Trussi took a breath as he approached the men.

"Good afternoon," he said brightly.

The three nodded toward him and replied, "Good afternoon."

He shook hands with all of them, making sure to smile. Trussi didn't waste any time and turned towards the blacksmith. "I am glad to see you here. I heard you recently lost your apprentice, and I was hoping to talk to you about taking his place."

The blacksmith raised his eyebrows as he looked him up and down. His hair and beard were salt-and-pepper colored, and the lines on his face were deep, showing the effects of a long, hard life. After a moment, he finally asked, "Boy, how old are you?"

"I'm seventeen, sir," Trussi answered boldly. He puffed up his chest, trying to look bigger than he already was.

The blacksmith rubbed his forehead in thought. "I don't know. An apprentice usually starts by the age of fourteen or fifteen. You're a bit old to start now."

Trussi wouldn't give up that easily. "Sir, I'm a fast learner. I have a powerful drive to do things correctly. I'm also a very hard worker, and I'm patient too." Okay, so that last bit was a stretch, but so what? Unfortunately, the blacksmith needed to be more convinced.

"Please, sir, give me a couple of days. If you don't think I can do this, I'll leave and never bother you again." Trussi hated begging, but there was no other option. He had to get this apprenticeship. "I am also strong. I can handle anything."

The blacksmith sighed. "Okay, fine. I'll try you out for one week. Be at my shop tomorrow morning. Early!"

Trussi shook his hand emphatically and thanked him. He hurried off home, each step full of energy and excitement. 'YES!' he cheered internally at his chance of becoming the blacksmith's apprentice! Trussi realized he didn't even know the blacksmith's name on the walk home. He had never formally introduced himself, though he had met the blacksmith several times previously. He shrugged his shoulders at this thought. Tomorrow he was going to start his apprenticeship. He'd learn his name then.

Once he reached his home, Trussi changed out of his Sunday clothes. His stomach grumbled in protest, reminding him he was hungry. The market was closed for the day, and he had forgotten to bring home any food yesterday. Luckily, Trussi knew the creek emptied into a large pond with plenty of fish to catch. It was a leisurely walk from his house, but it was the only option he knew to get food for the day. He gathered everything he needed and then headed for the pond.

Once he reached the stream, Trussi followed it. Once he arrived at the familiar pond, he looked around for a shaded, soft, muddy spot and found one nearby. Pulling out his hand shovel, he started digging for worms. After that, he baited his hook, and his line set out. Trussi relaxed and waited for his meal. It was only a short time till he had four good size fish. He started to pack up but remembered the widow and her children. He had not visited their doorstep with food in several days. Realizing this, he decided to continue fishing a bit longer.

He caught another fish before finally packing up and heading home. This catch was by far the best he had ever had here. Trussi saw that the end of the day was near and wanted to reach home before dark. Picking up his pace, he hastened home. He arrived home just before sunset. Despite his hunger, Trussi decided to deliver the fish to the widow before he fed himself. Once he quickly tucked his fishing supplies away, Trussi headed towards the widow's house with the three biggest fish he had.

Just as before, once he reached the widow's house, Trussi placed the fish in front of the door. He could hear the sounds of children from within, so he knew they were home. He knocked on the door and walked away, returning home to his fish dinner. After returning home, he lit the hearth and soon had a flame going. He roasted the remaining three fish over the fire, using some of the dried herbs he had on hand to add flavor.

Once he devoured the fish, Trussi's stomach was finally happy. After going to bed, thoughts of the blacksmith swam through his head. Sleep was restless at first. His stress was getting the best of him. Trussi needed to ensure he pleased the blacksmith to acquire the apprenticeship. So much was riding on this. When he finally relaxed, a dreamless, deep sleep engulfed him for the rest of the night.

CH. 3 COMPETITION

Trussi woke up early in the morning to roosters crowing and the sun rising. Hopping out of bed, he smiled, 'This is the day! My first day working with the blacksmith!' he thought happily. Trussi was ready and out the door immediately, heading to the blacksmith's shop. The blacksmith had said to be there early, so early he would be. His steps were quick, and he soon reached the shop in no time.

Once he arrived, Trussi noticed the chimney already had black smoke rising from its stacks. He walked up to the shop to knock on the front door. Just then, the door swung open.

"You're late," the blacksmith said. His tone expressed disappointment.

Trussi had no excuses to give. "I'm sorry, I thought I was early! I will be sure to come all the earlier tomorrow."

The blacksmith grunted and returned inside his shop, leaving the door open. Trussi tried to swallow but realized his throat was too dry. He was already off to a bad start. Following the blacksmith, they went into the back of the smoky workshop. Inside was large and had many windows to help ventilate and disperse the heat from the forge. The large forge was in the center of this room. It was already lit, with heat emanating from its core.

The blacksmith pointed to the forge, "This is the lifeblood of being a blacksmith. It takes a vast amount of coal to heat the forge properly, as it heats slowly." Looking Trussi in the eyes, he said intensely, "It must be lit early in the morning, or by the time it is hot enough to do any work, there will not be enough hours left to complete anything."

Trussi nodded his head in acknowledgment. "I understand."

The blacksmith waved a hand at one of the windows. "It is already getting hot. Open the windows to let in some fresh air." Trussi rushed over and opened every window as fast as he could. He wanted to be sure to satisfy the blacksmith again. At that moment, he decided he would do everything asked of him very quickly. Once completed, he returned to the blacksmith, who started heating several long iron bars in the forge.

The blacksmith looked up at Trussi, his eyes very serious. "Not everything involved with this job is a race. For now, you are to observe. Learn everything you can by watching. I may ask you to do a simple task, such as fetching water, but other than that, you are not to touch anything." He paused momentarily, "You can ask questions if you don't get in my way. By the end of the week, I will ask YOU questions about what I've shown you. If you cannot answer my questions, you will not continue and will not become my apprentice. Is that clear?"

"Very clear," Trussi replied firmly.

The blacksmith pointed at the far back door and said, "Good. Now go open the door for patrons to enter." Trussi ran over to the door and opened it immediately. And with that, the blacksmith began his work. Trussi never allowed his mind to wander and always kept his concentration. He paid close attention to everything the blacksmith did and said. He watched how he heated the iron bars, turning them just so, and how items were hammered, cooled, and handled. On occasion, Trussi would ask a question, and the blacksmith would give a brief, precise answer.

Several patrons came by to discuss with the blacksmith what they needed. One was a farmer who needed nails. He was building a barn for his growing herd of cattle. Another patron was a merchant who paid for replacement wheels for two of his carriages. The blacksmith would barter over fees, and once they were satisfied with the price, they would discuss a date to pick up the finished items. Trussi was curious if the blacksmith would ask about any of this. Regardless, he made sure to observe everything. He made a point to remember each discussion.

During these conversations, Trussi learned that the blacksmith's name was Ferraro. Ferraro spoke little but was always busy and always actively working. As the day passed, Trussi noticed Ferraro would recheck the measurements of completed items. He was constantly making sure he always did his work perfectly. After finishing the day's work, Ferraro prepared the material for tomorrow's work and started hammering some iron he had already been heating. That evening, Ferraro showed Trussi how to properly 'turn down' the forge so it would be ready the following day. Doing this ensured that the forge would not burn the shop down and could become easily lit in the morning. Trussi attentively soaked up every detail.

Once Trussi was dismissed, he headed straight for the pub. His steps felt light as air, and a smile brimmed across his face. He was excited to tell Giada all about his day. On entering the pub, Trussi sat at a small empty table. He made sure it was close to where Giada was serving. His stomach growled hungrily as the smell of food wafted through the air. He waited patiently for Giada, who was still busy with other tables.

She showed a brilliant smile once she saw him waiting. Her eagerness to hear about his day was evident on her face. She approached and then lightly placed her hand on top of his. He smiled back and then gently placed his other hand on hers.

"How did it go? Is the blacksmith going to make you his apprentice?" Giada questioned.

Trussi shook his head. "He hasn't decided yet. For now, I am to observe and learn. At the end of the week, he'll ask me questions about what I've learned. If I answer them correctly, I will become his apprentice." Giada beamed with delight at his response.

Trussi let out a sigh. "However, if I answer incorrectly, he will dismiss me. If this happens, I will not become his apprentice."

Giada looked at him intensely, "Then you must be sure to answer correctly."

Trussi nodded and returned her intense stare. "I will," he said to her expectant gaze.

Giada then smiled and placed a hand on her hip. "Okay. So what will it be tonight? We have stew, porridge, fresh bread, and roasted corn."

Trussi's heart sank. Only just now did he remember that he was out of money. After Sunday's tithing, he had nothing left. Trussi stood up and told her, "I'm sorry, Giada. I have no more money this week. I probably won't start getting paid until the blacksmith accepts me as an apprentice." He turned to leave with a saddened look and a hungry belly.

Giada quickly grabbed his arm. "Meet me at the back entrance." She whispered it so quietly he wasn't sure he heard her correctly. Before he could ask, she turned around and headed for the kitchen. Trussi quickly left the pub and headed to the back of the building. The back door suddenly opened, and Giada appeared holding a linen sack. She handed it to him and said, "Here, this is leftover food from yesterday. No one will miss it."

Trussi clasped her hand, kissing the back of it. "My precious Giada, grazie." He gazed into her eyes, forgetting about his hunger and the kind gift of food he now held. She blushed but did not pull away. He slowly leaned in closer.

Pausing momentarily, she finally said, "I need to return to serving tables."

Trussi nodded and released her soft sweet hand. With a smile and a slow turn, Giada disappeared into the pub. Placing a hand on his chest, he sighed deeply. 'She is not just beautiful, but she is also kind,' he thought. And with that thought, Trussi turned around and headed for home.

Once he got home and settled, he ate some of the precious food Giada had given him. He could have eaten more, but he wanted to save the rest for later. Cleaning himself up quickly, Trussi then went to bed. It was earlier than he was used to, but he wanted to get plenty of rest to wake up early for the blacksmith in the morning.

Falling asleep earlier proved more difficult than he thought it would. At first, Trussi just lay there, staring at the ceiling. Once he started thinking about everything that had happened for the day, he drifted off to sleep without even realizing it. Dreams of failing to become an apprentice made his sleep uneasy.

Trussi shifted in his bed, waking himself up. He looked outside, it was still dark, but the horizon was barely starting to lighten, implying that the sun would rise soon. 'I did it! I woke up early!' he thought triumphantly. Getting out of bed quickly, Trussi was ready and immediately headed to the blacksmith's shop. He walked briskly and was excited about being up earlier than usual.

As he arrived at the blacksmith shop entrance, Trussi saw Ferraro approaching the shop. He happily thought to himself, 'Yes! I am not late!' It wasn't until the blacksmith was unlocking the door to enter that Trussi noticed the boy that was with him. He followed them inside, shutting the door as the lighted lantern showed the way. The boy looked young. He looked to be fourteen or maybe fifteen years old. Trussi's heart sank deeply then.

Ferraro pointed to Trussi. "This is Trussi," he said, introducing him to the boy. Then he pointed at the boy. "This is Baccio." He headed over to start lighting the forge and continued explaining. "Baccio is an orphan. The preacher wanted me to take him in as an apprentice. At the end of the week, I'll ask you multiple questions about what you've observed. If you answer correctly, I'll choose you as my apprentice. You will be dismissed and sent away should you answer incorrectly."

He paused for a moment, then continued. "However, if you cannot answer those questions correctly, I won't hesitate to dismiss you. Don't assume that you can stay should you answer better than each other. I won't settle for less than perfection." Both Trussi and Baccio nodded their heads fervently in understanding.

Trussi realized he now had competition for the apprenticeship. Since this boy was an orphan, he would likely have strong determination and resolve to gain the apprentice's position. Though frustrated, Trussi gritted his teeth and decided he would have to have even more resolve than before. He decided there was no way he would let this orphan take his place as the apprentice.

Ferraro started his work, getting everything ready for the day. Trussi kept a vigil watch on him, mentally noting everything he did. Baccio also seemed to be very observant. Soon, Ferraro instructed Trussi to open the shop door as the day's first customer approached. Baccio occasionally asked questions, but other than that, he remained quiet. Trussi was taller than Baccio, so when they were observing the blacksmith, Trussi allowed him to stand in front without argument out of his courteous nature.

Occasionally Ferraro would send them on tasks or direct them to fetch certain supplies. After a while, he sent Baccio to fetch a pail of water. While doing that chore, he had Trussi shovel coal for the forge. Trussi was always quick to respond and wanted to be quick to complete any task asked of him. Baccio was just as swift but lacked muscle mass. Trussi had already finished shoveling coal, but Baccio had yet to return with the pail of water. Trussi was worried Baccio was struggling to retrieve the water.

Trussi had a concerning thought, 'If Baccio fails to return with the water soon, he may get dismissed. He pondered this a little more. If Baccio fails this early, then this could put the blacksmith in a foul mood. Trussi didn't want Ferraro to take any frustration out on himself. 'That could put me at risk of being also dismissed.' Trussi felt torn as he thought this. After a moment, Trussi decided he may need to help Baccio. He wanted to stay on Ferraro's good side as he was still determining the man's temperament. The blacksmith appeared occupied while speaking with a customer. So, Trussi slipped out quietly. Once he was outside, Trussi could see Baccio down the road. His heart sank as he saw him struggling with the water pail. The kid was trying as hard as he could. But, he was thin and gangly, having too little muscle to perform the simple task.

Trussi sighed. Despite his desire to get the apprenticeship, he couldn't stand to see the orphan fail on his first day. He trotted down the road to help the kid out. 'I must be an idiot!' he thought grudgingly to himself. No one in their right mind would help their competition! He reached Baccio quickly and grabbed the handle of the pail.

"Did the blacksmith send you?" Baccio huffed out, nearly breathless. "Is he mad at me?" The kid looked like he would burst into tears any second.

"No, he didn't send me. I came because I don't want him to get upset or frustrated." Trussi then started to pull on the pail to carry its weight.

"No!" Baccio demanded. "It's my task! If I cannot complete it, then I'll be dismissed! I won't let you take it!" His eyes went from sad to angry in an instant.

Trussi sighed again. "Fine," he said. "I'll help you carry it for just a little while. When we arrive at the shop, I'll let go. The blacksmith will see that only you completed the task."

Baccio huffed and still looked angry but didn't argue. Trussi held the handle with the boy, carrying most of its weight. True to his word, Trussi let go of the pail once they reached the shop. Trussi entered the shop first and returned to his place quickly and quietly. Baccio also entered the shop, carrying the water just as the blacksmith finished with the customer.

"Place it over there." Ferraro pointed to the corner of the room. Baccio took the pail over to the corner, breathing heavily every step of the way. Once done, he quickly wiped the sweat off his forehead, trying not to look so exhausted.

The rest of the day went by quickly. Ferraro closed the shop and repeated the final tasks he had done the night before. Trussi observed everything Ferraro did attentively, making sure he missed nothing. Like before, Trussi and Baccio were dismissed, and they left with Ferraro securing the lock. As he was leaving, Trussi's stomach growled at him with hunger. Despite his empty stomach, as he left to go to the pub, there was only one thought on his mind: Giada.

There was still plenty of daylight left as he arrived at the pub. Trussi entered and found a small empty table to sit at and wait. Giada soon spotted Trussi and walked over to his table. She smiled wide when greeting him, showing her dimples. He loved those dimples.

"How did today go?" She asked as her eyes searched his expectantly.

Trussi smiled back at her. "I think it went well. I completed several tasks that the blacksmith asked me to do. I also kept vigil watch on him, working hard to ensure every detail was committed to memory."

She placed her hand on his. "Good. You'll be the blacksmith's apprentice before you know it." Trussi's eyebrows furrowed as he thought of Baccio. Giada saw the concern on his face. "What is it?" she asked.

Trussi took a deep breath. "The preacher brought an orphan boy to work with the blacksmith today, hoping that he might take him on as an apprentice." Giada's grip on his hand tightened. "He's skin-and-bones. A boy, fourteen years of age at most. But he's eager to learn the trade." Giada nodded for him to continue, preparing herself for the bad news. "The blacksmith said that either of us could become his apprentice or neither of us. It depends on how well we answer his questions at the end of the week."

Giada was silent as she processed this new information. She finally nodded her head. "Well then, you must be sure to answer all his questions. Show him how eager you are to learn the trade."

Trussi nodded his head in agreement. "That is why I am here. I have to awaken early in the morning, before sunrise. Which means I will need to be in bed early each night. If I do not rise early, I will be tardy again." Trussi swallowed hard, finding it dreadful to say the following words. "I don't think I'll be coming by here to see you for the rest of the week. I need to be in bed as early as I can." He looked away from Giada, finding it hard to say these unwanted words while looking into those beautiful eyes.

"But at the end of the week, I'll come back. I'll let you know whether or not I got the apprenticeship."

Giada nodded her sad understanding, disappointment showing through her lovely features. She gently touched his shoulder and whispered, "Can I help you somehow? Do you need anything? More food, perhaps?" At the mere suggestion of food, Trussi's stomach growled up at him. Giada giggled at the sound. "I take it that's a 'yes' then." She paused and looked around. "Meet me at the back again." And with that, she walked away, heading for the kitchen.

Trussi left and headed towards the back entrance like he had the night before. Just like before, the door opened and revealed Giada. She stood there holding a linen sack with food once again. It appeared larger and fuller than it had last night. Trussi scooped up her hand, lightly placing a tender kiss. "Until we meet again, my sweet Giada." She smiled deeply.

"Until we meet again, sweet Trussi. I will pray for your success!" Giada quickly handed him the linen sack and disappeared as she returned to the pub without another word. He turned around to head home. Then he heard a sound that sent a disturbing shiver down his spine. Someone was watching him!

"Who's there?" He called out forcefully. Trussi's fist clenched as he made his voice loud and confident. If someone was going to rob him, they had another thing coming. A small figure stepped out of the shadowy trash area. It was Baccio, and he was holding a partial loaf of moldy bread. His large eyes were open wide with fear as he revealed himself.

"What are you doing here?" Trussi asked, his voice still sounding angry.

"I... I was hungry." Baccio's voice came out shakily. He lowered his eyes, showing his shame.

Trussi felt irritated at this odd intrusion. "Isn't the preacher or the blacksmith housing you? I would assume one of them should be feeding you."

Baccio shook his head. "The preacher doesn't have room for me. That's why he took me to the blacksmith." He paused for a moment, shuffling his feet nervously. "The blacksmith won't house me until he accepts me as an apprentice."

Trussi's fist relaxed. He hadn't realized he was still clenching. The kid's words sank in as he realized what he was saying. "So you have nowhere to go, no family at all?" Baccio shook his head. He could see this boy was thin as a rake and hungry, making him appear even younger. Trussi sighed deeply. "Kid, how old are you?"

Baccio perked up, standing as tall as he could. "I'm thirteen." He was looking Trussi square in the eyes. "But this winter, I'll be fourteen." His eyes were intense, showing nothing but a spark of determination.

Trussi sighed again. He felt heartbroken for the kid; he certainly did. But this was not his problem! 'I have many issues already. Not only that, but this kid is my competition.' Trussi was about to continue to head home but discovered he couldn't take a single step. He closed his eyes in frustration. No, he thought, leaving him here wouldn't be right. Thoughts of his grandmother seeped into his mind. She was as kind as she was firm. What would she want Trussi to do? He didn't have to answer that. He already knew.

"Fine," He sighed. "You can stay with me." Baccio gave him a confused look. Trussi waved his hand and the sack of food. "I have food I can share with you. And there is an extra bed if you want it." He took several steps before he continued. "It's this way if you want to come." And with that, Trussi started walking home. It was up to the kid to follow. If Baccio didn't accompany him, it wasn't Trussi's fault.

It didn't take long for Trussi to hear the light footsteps of Baccio following him. Turning around, he saw the kid still holding the moldy bread. "Don't eat that!" Trussi took the bread out of the kid's hands.

Baccio protested. "Hey, that's mine!" He flung his arms at Trussi, trying to get the bread back.

Trussi held him back with ease. "Calm down, kid." He held up the sack again. "I have plenty of food I can share. And it's not moldy." He then chucked the moldy bread into one of the dark corridors they were walking past.

Baccio calmed himself but still looked upset. He eyed Trussi suspiciously as if he would do something terrible at any moment. Despite this, they continued walking until they reached his house. Dusk was approaching, and Trussi knew they would need firewood.

Turning towards Baccio, Trussi said, "This is my home." It felt odd saying it out loud. As he entered, he waved at the kid, inviting him in.

Trussi put the food sack on the counter and shuffled through the items. He selected a small piece of bread and some cooked meat and then handed them to Baccio. The kid seized the items without hesitation and immediately started scarfing them down. Trussi grabbed the kid's hands to slow him down. "Hey!" He said sternly. "Slow down, or you'll choke." The kid nodded at him but didn't seem to slow down very much. Trussi retrieved a cup and filled it with water from a pitcher on the counter. He then handed the cup to Baccio.

"Here, drink this before you choke yourself."

The kid's mouth was so full he couldn't speak. He took the cup readily and started gulping the water. Thankfully, the water carried the contents of his mouth down his throat. 'He didn't choke, thank goodness.' Trussi thought, relieved. It wasn't long before the kid devoured the morsels of food given to him. Trussi contemplated for a moment. When was the last time this kid had eaten? It had likely been a long time. Baccio soon refilled his empty cup. While doing this, Trussi could see him looking absentmindedly over at the linen sack of food.

Before the kid could say anything, Trussi cut him off. "We need some firewood." He glanced outside. Dusk had just set in. "Once we're all done, we'll come back here, start a fire in the hearth, and eat until we're full." He looked down at the kid, placing a hand on his shoulder. Baccio nodded his head and smiled. Bread crumbs were still stuck in the corners of his mouth, causing Trussi to smile. 'Damn, this kid is so likable.' Trussi thought cheerfully. He led the kid to the back side of the house and retrieved his ax.

Trussi first showed him how he lined up the raw wood. Baccio copied Trussi precisely. Next, Trussi demonstrated how to correctly hold the ax handle and how to swing it without causing injury to himself. After chopping several pieces of wood, Trussi handed the ax to the kid.

"Show me," Trussi said as he pointed to the wood.

Baccio swallowed hard but took the ax firmly. His first several swings were awkward and could have been more relaxed. So, Trussi helped him to adjust his stance and his swing. Finally, the kid improved his swing. They took turns until there was plenty of wood for the rest of the week. Once finished, Trussi pulled the pail up from the well. Both of them washed away the sweat and stinkiness they had accumulated.

After that, they both carried wood inside the home. While doing this, Trussi's stomach growled hungrily. He had not fed himself yet and was famished. Turning to the kid, Trussi caught Baccio eyeing the linen sack again. A smile spread across Trussi's face. "Okay, it's time to eat."

Trussi opened the linen sack, reviewing its contents more thoroughly now. He was going to need at least five days' supply of food. Looking over at Baccio, Trussi groaned to himself. He realized they would need to feed the kid as well. 'Great." He thought to himself sarcastically. 'Another mouth to feed.' He sighed. What he had in this sack and what he had reserved from yesterday would not be enough for both of them. Trussi decided that he would have to take the kid fishing.

Trussi divided the rest of the food out. Trussi gave Baccio a portion of the food, and without hesitation, Baccio began hastily eating again. Sitting by the Hearth, surrounded by warmth, the two ate their food. Once he finished, he took Baccio to his grandmother's room. No one had slept in her bed after her passing, but letting the kid sleep on the floor didn't seem right. After showing the kid to the room, Trussi bid him goodnight.

Just before going to his bed, Trussi returned to where the remaining food was and placed it on a high shelf, keeping it hidden. He didn't fully trust the kid yet. The temptation to sneak food might prove too much for him. Trussi then went to his bed, falling asleep with ease. His dreams were a mixture of his grandmother and the blacksmith. Trussi found it funny how his grandmother bossed the blacksmith around as if he were her grandson. He chuckled at the scene and continued sleeping deeply through the night.

CH. 4   INVALUABLE LESSONS

Trussi awoke in the morning and was happy it was still dark outside, with the horizon line barely showing signs of the sunrise soon to come. Good, he thought. He had woken up early again, and he let out a sigh of relief. After leaving his room, he woke up Baccio, still sleeping, half covered in the blanket and half off the bed.

"Dawn is nearly here. We need to get to the blacksmith's early." Trussi didn't wait for the kid to respond. He hoisted him up by the arm and got Baccio to his feet.

They left shortly after, walking at a brisk pace. They reached the blacksmith's shop just as Ferraro was unlocking his door to enter. They entered together and awaited instructions. Trussi felt considerably less nervous this day than he had before. During the workday, Ferraro continued to ask Baccio or Trussi to perform simple tasks.

Trussi made sure to ask questions, especially when Ferraro began using a tool or instrument he had not previously seen before. Baccio also asked questions, and Trussi liked this. Baccio seemed to have questions Trussi had yet to think to ask. Like the previous day, when Ferraro completed all the work, Trussi and Baccio were dismissed. Trussi noticed Ferraro had appeared less agitated and slightly more pleasant to be around. He wondered if Ferraro was considering him for the apprenticeship. This thought made him smile the whole walk home. Once the two reached home, Trussi went to the back of the house, gathering his fishing gear.

"Today we are going fishing!" he announced to Baccio.

Baccio then slumped and shuffled his feet nervously. "I..." He swallowed hard, trying to find his voice. "... I have never fished before." Trussi had figured as much. He placed his hand on Baccio's shoulder, and the boy looked at him nervously.

"It's not that hard. I can teach you." He paused for a moment, thinking. "You will need to listen carefully and be quiet around the pond. You can ask questions, but you mustn't be loud, or you will scare away the fish. Should that happen, there won't be any supper tonight." Baccio nodded his understanding. Trussi then handed the kid some of the fishing items to carry. From there, they both made their way toward the large pond.

During the walk, Baccio often skipped, grabbed a stick, or tossed a rock playfully. Trussi wondered if this was what it felt like to have a younger brother. Someone to help, someone to teach. It was a different feeling this way, but he decided he liked it. Trussi smiled at this thought, but the moment was fleeting. The realization that the end of the week would soon arrive ruined the moment. Once the end of the week was here, one or both of them could lose the blacksmith's apprenticeship job. Should Baccio be granted the apprentice position, he would be housed by the blacksmith. Trussi would not only lose the kid's company but Giada's as well. He had no desire to be alone again. However, if Trussi got the apprenticeship, the kid might hate him for that, leaving him anyway out of spite.

Once they reached the pond, Trussi pushed these thoughts out of his head. He needed to focus on one thing at a time. For now, they need to catch enough fish to eat tonight and last until the end of the week. Trussi showed Baccio the best places to dig for worms. Once they had plenty, he showed him how to hook the worms so they wouldn't fall off in the water. Lastly, Trussi showed Baccio where to cast the fishing line for the best catch.

Baccio was inquisitive. He would ask more questions than he had with the blacksmith. Trussi couldn't help but laugh, finding it humorous and appreciative to have so many questions to answer. He even caught Baccio smiling from time to time. It didn't take long for Trussi to reel in the first fish. Trussi showed him how to carefully grab the fish so he wouldn't get the fish's spikes embedded in his hand. The kid caught on quickly and handled the next two fish he caught perfectly.

Trussi decided it was best to head home after that, as he wanted to return to bed early. Once they reached his home, he showed the kid how to stow the gear. He then had the kid fetch a pail of water as he got the fire in the hearth going. Once the kid brought in the water pail, Trussi had him pour it into the large pot and place it over the fire. Trussi cut up the few vegetables he had set aside and added them to the heating water. He took the kid to the backyard again, showing him where to look for the wild spices in the garden. These were the same spices planted and used by his grandmother. She had taught Trussi what to use when he was young.

They brought the spices in and added them to the pot. Trussi then used a sharp knife to gut and debone one of the fish, carefully showing the kid every step. Handing the sharp knife to Baccio, he had him repeat the process on another fish. The kid struggled with the fish, and Trussi took over to prevent him from ruining what was to be a big part of the meal. He showed him the process again, a little slower this time.

Trussi handed the kid the knife again and had him retry on the third and last fish. Baccio did better this time and only needed a little assistance. Trussi added the meat to the pot with the fish heads for flavor. Trussi then took Baccio and the fish scraps to the back of the house. He showed Baccio how to bury these items deep, serving a dual purpose. Doing this helped fertilize the soil so the garden would grow better and also helped not attract rats. Once fully disposed of, they returned inside, where the smell of stew filled the air and enticed their bellies to grumble.

Trussi filled two bowls with the steaming aromatic stew. They had no difficulty consuming the soup, and their bowls were soon empty. Trussi had hoped to save the remainder of the soup for the next day. However, Baccio still looked hungry. And, if he was being honest with himself, he was too. He went ahead and scooped out the remaining stew in the bowls. They ate heartily, though slower. Once finished, Trussi let out a sigh of contentment. His stomach finally felt full and satisfied. Baccio also let out the same sigh and smiled while rubbing his happily filled belly.

The sun was setting outside, and Trussi knew he needed to sleep. Looking over, he saw Baccio was already yawning as he headed to bed. While in bed, thoughts of Giada floated around Trussi's mind, preventing his much-desired quick sleep. It had only been one day since he had last seen her, and he yearned to see her smile.

Trussi sighed deeply. If he didn't fall asleep soon, he could wake up late, which would upset Ferraro. Luckily, Trussi knew of something that always put him to sleep. Getting up, he went to get the only book in his possession, The Golden Mountain. He took it to his bed, lit a candle, and read. Trussi wasn't sure when sleep finally found him. When it did, he had dreams filled with adventure and treasure.

Trussi awoke suddenly in the morning. Baccio was next to him, shaking his arm. "It's almost sunrise! We need to get to the shop!" Trussi nodded, still not fully awake yet. He blinked several times as Baccio's words sank in. Looking out the window, he realized it wasn't dark as the sun was awakening. He jolted up quickly.

"We need to leave. Now!" Trussi stammered as he got to his feet. They headed out quickly. Trussi was grateful Baccio had gotten up when he did. Otherwise, they would have both been late. They made no effort to talk with each other as they were jogging along the road. Trussi couldn't help but think of why Baccio would wake him up. He could have left Trussi to sleep, gaining favor with Ferraro. But instead, the kid woke him up, so they would both be on time. Trussi couldn't help but like this kid more and more.

It took time to reach the shop. Luck was on their side as they arrived at the same time as Ferraro. Trussi and Baccio were gasping lightly for breath but were fine again shortly after arriving. Trussi didn't want Ferraro to know they were nearly late. Luckily Ferraro appeared not to notice and continued his morning duties as usual.

Ferraro had more tasks for Trussi and Baccio to complete on this day. They both hurried to complete each task asked of them. Trussi noticed Ferraro still appeared in a better mood and was hopeful it meant he was strongly considering him for the apprenticeship.

The end of the day quickly came as they completed all their tasks without complaint. Trussi looked forward to taking Baccio out fishing again. Once there, Baccio performed better, hooking the worm properly without instruction and casting in the correct areas. They caught the first four fish rather quickly. Baccio, thinking they had finished, started packing up. However, Trussi had something else in mind and instructed Baccio to continue fishing for more.

The kid appeared confused but did as instructed. They caught four additional fish before it was time to head back home. It was the best catch Trussi had ever had. He expressed how proud he was of Baccio and complimented his technique. The kid was a natural fisherman. Once they arrived home, they again stowed the gear. However, instead of returning inside to prepare the meal, Trussi headed to the front of the house. Trussi had taken four fish they had caught with him and was preparing to head to the widow's house.

"Before we cook our dinner, I have something I need to do first," he told Baccio. He was reluctant to tell Baccio what he intended to do, so he just started towards the town.

Baccio followed quickly with an irritated look on his face. "What are you going to do?!" The kid's voice sounded more angry than inquisitive. He pointed at the fish Trussi held and loudly stated, "Half of those fish are mine!"

Trussi sighed, slowly shaking his head. He hadn't told anyone about the food he occasionally left at the widow's house. No one had asked him to do it. Trussi had noticed the family struggling and felt that helping them was the right thing to do.

Trussi looked back at Baccio, who had his fist clenched and eyes furrowed angrily.

"Look, kid. I am not stealing these fish." He paused, unsure why he was reluctant to talk about what he was doing.

Trussi walked over to the kid and handed him the fish. "Here. You can help me with the chore I have." He then placed a hand on the kid's shoulder, raising the other hand towards the town.

Baccio eyed him suspiciously but followed him anyway. Shortly, they approached the widow's house. Trussi pointed to the front door. "This family lost their father earlier this summer." He looked at Baccio somberly. "I saw the widow and her three children struggle. They have no family to help them, and the kids often have no food."

Baccio looked at the door as the anger dwindled from his face. Trussi continued quietly, "No one asked me to do this. But when I can, I put food on their doorstep. I knock on the door, but I don't stay because," He paused, not knowing why he never stayed. He seldom talked to others, as conversation for him was often awkward. "... because I wouldn't know what to say."

Trussi looked the kid in the eyes as he took the fish. Baccio watched Trussi intensely. He looked young again, less hardened and calloused than before. Trussi then turned around and placed the fish on the front door entrance. He knocked and walked away, taking Baccio with him. As they walked home, Trussi felt awkward and couldn't tell what Baccio was thinking.

Once they reached home, Trussi paused before going in. "Look, Baccio. I don't expect you to understand..." The kid cut him off with a sudden hug. His embrace startled Trussi, who remained motionless as Baccio wrapped his arms around him. Trussi felt awkward as he was unsure what to do.

Baccio let go and looked up at him. His voice seemed to waver as he said, "I have never had a father..." Several tears fell from his eyes, causing his voice to falter. He tried to wipe them away, smearing the dirt on his face as he continued, "...but if I did, I wish he were someone like you." His voice cracked at the end, and more tears fell from his eyes.

Trussi felt a lump in his throat. He barely knew the kid, and he already felt like an older brother to him. Trussi returned the hug, holding back tears that threatened to fall at any moment. "I never had a brother..." He paused as a tear defied his will and streaked down his face "... but if I did, I wish he were someone like you." Baccio hugged him back. At this moment, Trussi felt as if they were honestly brothers. Their embrace ended momentarily, and they headed back inside the house.

Trussi didn't waste any time and started the dinner fire. He then started skewering some vegetables for roasting. While Trussi was doing this, he directed Baccio as he was preparing the fish. Only this time, he instructed him to leave them whole for roasting. The kid did a decent job with the fish considering it was only his second time handling them. Trussi rubbed some spices on the fish, skewered them, and then started roasting them over the fire with the vegetables.

Once fully cooked, Trussi showed Baccio how to remove the cooked meat from the fish while separating the bones. It didn't take long for the meal to become devoured as they were both famished. Trussi may have even burned his tongue a little as he had not allowed his food to cool enough before eating.

They both went to bed shortly after cleaning up. Lying there, Trussi started thinking about Giada once again. He hoped he would soon become the blacksmith's apprentice, and then he could court her. His heart pounded deeply just thinking about it. Soon, he started thinking about Baccio. Trussi decided that when he got the apprenticeship, he would talk with the kid and convince him to stay. Baccio felt decidedly like a brother to him, and Trussi didn't want to lose him any more than he wanted to lose Giada. No matter what it took, Trussi decided he would convince Baccio to stay with him. They worked so well together that it just made sense for them both. Trussi took in a big, relaxing, deep breath. Everything appeared to be falling into place for him. His heart felt light, and it wasn't long until sleep stole him away and carried him through the night.

Trussi discovered his waking up early in the morning was

getting easier. It was still dark outside, but he felt less groggy than the last several mornings. 'I must be getting used to waking up early!' Trussi happily decided. He went to wake up Baccio but discovered he was already up. Baccio smiled sleepily at him but wasted no time getting ready. They headed out together and arrived on time again, helping the blacksmith open the shop.

As the day went on, Ferraro started talking more thoroughly about blacksmithing. He also explained why he was doing every step. His explanations had become more in-depth than it was previously. Trussi was fascinated and listened intently to the vivid discussions of heating iron and other metal. He loved learning what intense heating did to the different metals. Also, differing heating and cooling techniques gave iron many unique properties. Ferraro was an experienced master in his craft.

Trussi started imagining himself as the blacksmith. He saw himself heating and bending iron into different shapes for various tools. He could see himself using the large, heavy hammer and anvil, creating marvelous items the townsfolk needed. Trussi then blinked for a moment, realizing he had been daydreaming.

'No! I have to pay attention! No time for daydreams!' Trussi thought, reprimanding himself. Trussi quickly glanced around, looking for Ferraro. Luckily, he was bartering with a customer at the moment. Trussi let out a sigh of relief and was grateful it seemed as though he had not missed anything important.

Trussi kept all his focus on Ferraro for the rest of the day. He refused to allow more daydreams to distract him from his job for Giada. With him focusing so intently, he had forgotten about Baccio. Trussi finally noticed him at the end of the day when Ferraro dismissed them. They were both hungry by the time they got home. Unfortunately, once they arrived, Trussi remembered that no food remained from the previous meal. There was also no more food from the reserve in the linen sack either.

They needed to fish again, so they gathered the fishing gear and headed out. They tried fishing with impatient bellies.

Unfortunately, as the hours passed, they realized their lucky streak seemed to have run dry. The fish weren't biting much. Trussi had hoped they would catch extra fish before the last of the market stands were closed. This way, he could barter for potatoes or corn to go with their meal. By the time they needed to leave for home, they had only caught two fish.

After stowing the gear, Trussi decided it was time to show Baccio how to get the hearth going. Trussi brought him over, showing Baccio how to tend the hearth fire. It was the same way his grandmother had taught him. Once a healthy fire was glowing, they prepared the meager catch of the day and roasted the fish over the open flames.

Despite being hungry, Trussi found he could barely eat. He knew the next day was Saturday, and the blacksmith would decide the apprenticeship. Baccio's mind must have been on the blacksmith also, as he ate his meal considerably slower than usual. Trussi, unable to finish his small meal, handed it over to Baccio. Neither said much, and Trussi hated the silence. However, Trussi wasn't sure what to say either, so the silence persisted into the night.

When finally heading for bed, Trussi turned to Baccio and touched his shoulder. "Sleep well, Baccio." He wanted to say something uplifting but couldn't find the right words. Lying in his bed, Trussi found himself wide awake and staring at the wall all night. He wanted to sleep, but the weight of the next day kept him from getting rest. Stressful thoughts floated around his troubled mind.

Thoughts like 'What if Baccio hates me after I get the apprenticeship? I don't want him to leave! What if the blacksmith rejects me and picks Baccio instead? I won't have a trade or Giada! I can't live without Giada, I just can't!' kept running through his restless mind.

Trussi tossed and turned in bed for a while. Sleep eventually found him, but his dreams were restless and caused him to wake often. Frustrated and stressed, Trussi kept tossing and turning until he could see the faint glowing line outside the dawning sunrise soon to come.

CH. 5 APPRENTICESHIP

Trussi went to wake up Baccio but found he was already awake. Baccio's eyes looked tired, and Trussi figured the kid probably had as much sleep as he did. Neither of them said much during their walk to the blacksmith's shop. They arrived just as Ferraro arrived. They all entered and started the workday. Trussi started to help Baccio open the shop like normal, but Ferraro called him over to the forge.

Ferraro touched Trussi's shoulder firmly and asked, "Do you think you could light it?" Trussi nodded his head slowly.

Ferraro motioned with his hand towards the forge and stepped back. Trussi stepped forward, swallowing hard. He replayed every step in his mind, knowing the exact process. Trussi began lighting the forge with ease.

As Trussi worked on the forge, he noticed Ferraro talking with Baccio. Trussi couldn't hear the conversation but saw Baccio nodding, and then he left the shop. 'Must be completing a task of some sort!?' he thought. Trussi shook his head then. He needed to focus on what he was doing rather than whatever Baccio was doing.

He continued with the forge, concentrating on each step. The process was slow, but eventually, the forge was heating correctly. Ferraro's face remained neutral, and Trussi couldn't tell if he had pleased him. Baccio returned shortly after. He was carrying two water pails and was clearly out of breath. Sweat was heavily beading on his forehead at that effort.

The day was filled with the blacksmith asking Baccio or Trussi questions or instructing one of them to perform a task. Ferraro always remained neutral and did not indicate if anything they had said or done was correct. Trussi was becoming frustrated as he couldn't tell whether or not he was doing well.

Customers came picking up items or placing a new order with Ferraro. Even when Ferraro was with customers, he carefully watched Trussi and Baccio all day. Trussi made sure he was always active, working hard throughout the day. Time seemed to move slowly, and Trussi thought the day would never end. Despite all his efforts, Trussi's exhaustion was weighing him down. He could see Baccio's growing exhaustion too. Despite this, Trussi was still determined to do his best.

The end of the day finally arrived. Trussi was so nervous that his stomach clenched up in knots. He was afraid he would vomit at any moment. Baccio didn't look much better.

Ferraro approached them both, saying, "You boys go home and get some rest. After church tomorrow, we'll meet here. I'll tell you my decision of who will become my apprentice." Trussi nodded but felt the weight on his shoulders steepening.

Both Baccio and Trussi left disheartened. They both felt disappointed and scared when they realized they wouldn't know the results until late tomorrow. Baccio must have felt the same way as the usual fast walk home was slow and sedate. After barely eating anything yesterday, Trussi realized he was not only exhausted but famished as well. The nausea was no longer present and left him with intense hunger. He looked over at Baccio and imagined he was probably just as starved.

Trussi had only two options for food. He could try fishing again or go to see Giada. However, he decided that he couldn't ask Giada for more food. He needed to be able to provide for her, not the other way around. Since asking Giada for additional food was not an option, Trussi knew he needed to fish again. He reached out and placed a hand on Baccio's shoulder. He felt Baccio jump at his touch but then relax as the kid looked up at him.

"We should hurry. I know you're exhausted, and so am I, but we need to go fishing, or neither of us will have any food tonight."

Baccio nodded his head, and they picked up the pace. They reached home in a respectable time and gathered up the fishing gear. They made their way to the familiar pond and immediately started fishing. Trussi was grateful luck was on their side, and they caught five fish quickly.

Trussi turned to Baccio, "Baccio, I have a question for you. I know you are just as hungry as I am, but I have no money for the tithe at church tomorrow." Baccio looked at him, his eyes looking exhausted. Trussi continued hesitantly. "We can take these fish home and fill our bellies..." Trussi paused for a moment, taking a deep breath. He was still determining how much Baccio trusted him.

"... or, I can take three fish to the marketplace and trade them for some money for the tithing tomorrow. You can stay here to try to catch more fish. We can meet at home and eat these two fish plus whatever more you might catch." Trussi placed a hand on Baccio's shoulder. "You decide what we should do. I won't make you do something you are not sure about."

Baccio closed his eyes for a moment and sucked in a deep breath. Finally, he nodded his head. "You should take the fish to the marketplace. If we don't have any money to tithe, then we won't receive any blessings."

Trussi hugged the kid and tousled his hair playfully. "Alright, it's settled. I'll meet you back at the house. Don't stay more than an hour, or it'll be too dark to see your way home safely."

Baccio nodded, then handed him four of the fish. Trussi furrowed his eyebrows in confusion. "But I only need..."

Baccio cut him off, "Take four, as we both need money for the tithing tomorrow. I'll catch more fish for dinner. Trust me." Trussi smiled, nodding at Baccio's words about them both. Baccio was thinking of them possibly as a family. Or perhaps as brothers, and that thought Trussi joy. He took the four fish and headed back to town. He was hasty, as the day was getting late. Trussi hated leaving Baccio alone but knew he could trust the kid.

Trussi made it to the marketplace just in time. Several stands were closing up, but a few were still open. He went to the one with the most vegetables and produce. From there, he proceeded to barter with the stand owner. Trussi looked over some of the stand's excess produce that was beginning to rot. These items were easier to barter over. Trussi not only got the money for the tithing, but he got a bushel of potatoes and a few other vegetables. From there, he headed home quickly.

Once Trussi made it home, he looked around, finding Baccio wasn't there yet. Trussi didn't want to wait, as his hunger was immense. He made a snack of a carrot as he prepared dinner. Once the pot was boiling, he quickly diced up and added the vegetables. Soon, with the herbs he added, the stew started to smell glorious.

Then Trussi started to worry as it was getting very dark outside, and Baccio had not yet returned home. He decided he had better head to the pond to find Baccio. What if the poor kid had gotten lost? He would never be able to find his way back while it was so dark. Worry permeated his thoughts as Trussi started to head out towards the pond. He knew it would be hard to find the kid. Just as he got to the end of his backyard, Trussi heard the rustling sounds of someone walking. He headed towards the sound and was relieved to see it was Baccio.

As Baccio approached him, a big wide grin filled his face. Once he got closer, Trussi saw Baccio holding a string of four fish. Trussi couldn't help but let out a burst of laughter. Both relief and pride overflowed him! The kid was not only okay, but he had caught more fish! After putting everything away, they added the fish to the boiling pot.

The wonderful aroma wafting up from the stew made both their stomachs grumble with hunger. Once Trussi served dinner, they slurped up the soup hastily, not bothering to use spoons. It took only a short time, and both refilled their bowls hastily. The second bowl of soup went down with little effort. Trussi let out a contented sigh as his belly finally felt satisfied. He put his bowl down on the counter and looked into the pot. He was glad to see plenty of stew left for the next day's meal.

Baccio, with his belly full, let out a big yawn. Trussi was exhausted and yawned also. He patted Baccio's shoulder and wished him good night. They both headed to bed, not saying much to each other. Trussi flopped onto his bed, too tired to think, and fell asleep instantly.

In the morning, the ringing of church bells woke the boys up. Trussi got up, as did Baccio, slowly at first. Trussi showed Baccio some stretches to help with the muscle aches and moving around soon became less achy. After that, they cleaned up and headed out for church. Walking to church was done leisurely, and Trussi found it enjoyable not having to rush to their destination. He also noticed that Baccio looked much better than the previous day. The meal and sleep did him some good as well. Once they reached the church, they entered with the rest of the townsfolk.

Everyone settled in while Baccio stayed towards the back with Trussi. They did their morning prayers, and the preacher did his Sermon as usual. Once the preacher finished the Sermon, everyone lined up for tithing. Trussi gave Baccio half the money from bartering at the marketplace. He had less than his usual amount for the tithing, but Trussi didn't care. He was grateful to have something to give. Even this minor amount was better than nothing.

After giving their tithes and receiving their blessings, Baccio and Trussi went to the gathering area. Trussi hadn't seen Giada for five days and was anxious to talk with her. He looked around and soon found her beautiful dimpled face and smile. She was with her parents as they were talking to the local baker.

Trussi approached them from the side, not wanting to interfere with her parent's conversation. Once Giada saw him, her face lit up with a large beautiful smile. She took several small steps moving away from her parents. She had only moved slightly, but it was enough for a private conversation. Giada lifted her hand for Trussi to hold. He took her hand, trying to be as discreet as possible.

"Did you get the apprenticeship?" Giada whispered.

Trussi sighed deeply. "Not yet. I am supposed to meet the blacksmith at his shop today after church. I'll find out then." Giada squeezed his hand with excitement. "I know the pub will be closed tonight, so I won't be able to tell you till tomorrow."

Giada wrinkled her nose and sighed. She nodded at him, a faint smile reforming in the corners of her lips. Just as Trussi was about to lean in close, Giada's parents ended their conversation with the baker, and she was whisked away from him. His heart fluttered as he watched her walk away. He memorized her wondrous form with each step as she disappeared from his view. Trussi realized he had forgotten about Baccio. Luckily he was nearby looking for Ferraro. Trussi also looked for Ferraro and discovered him speaking with the preacher. Trussi decided to head for the shop rather than interrupt his conversation. Baccio followed after him, and they walked unhurriedly together. Trussi found the walk to be relaxing then. And, despite the stress of coming news, Trussi felt good about the day. He was well fed, well rested, and ready to take on the day, whatever came of it. Baccio appeared to be feeling better as well. His stride was far lighter and perkier than yesterday.

They made it to the shop, though no one was there yet. It wasn't unexpected, and Trussi sat in the shade to relax while they waited. Baccio proceeded to pester a frog that had lost its way. Trussi chuckled to himself at this sight. About an hour passed when Ferraro appeared at the shop. He waved at the boys to enter, and suddenly Trussi found his feet were heavy and his heart pounded hard in his chest. 'This is it!' he thought and entered the shop slowly.

The blacksmith took them to the back and stood facing both of them. "You both have done well this past week." He paused, looking at each of them individually. "I want you to know this was not an easy decision." Ferraro took a deep breath, his face remaining neutral. Trussi couldn't tell what was going to happen. It felt as though his insides wanted to burst out, and his skin was the only thing holding everything back.

The blacksmith turned to Baccio and laid a hand on his shoulder. "You are eager to learn and careful with each task you complete. You also never give up, no matter how difficult the task is. Baccio, I'd like to offer you the apprentice position. If that is what you want."

Baccio's face lit up, and his eyes seemed to sparkle. It nearly looked like the kid would cry from pure joy. "Yes! Yes, it is what I want!"

Trussi's heart sank. His stomach knotted up, and he felt like he would vomit. He found himself unable to breathe. It was as if the entire world around him was falling apart. Ferraro turned to Trussi, placing his other hand on his shoulder.

"Trussi..." Upon hearing his name, Trussi tried to look up but couldn't lift his head. "...you are an eager learner as well. You are as kind as you are strong, which is not a common combination. You also never give up. I would also like to offer you the apprentice position. If that is what you want."

Trussi needed to find out if he heard him right. He finally breathed in some air and looked up at Ferraro. Ferraro had a twisted smile as if he knew he had just put him through hell.

"Did you just offer the apprenticeship to me also?" His words came out quiet and unsure.

Ferraro nodded his head. "I can have more than one apprentice if I wish, and you both did everything to my expectations. The apprenticeship is yours if you want it."

Trussi nodded his head fervently. "Yes, yes! I want it!" His voice carried the excitement he felt. He shook Ferraro's hand aggressively and then turned to Baccio, who was wiping away tears of joy. Trussi grabbed him, giving him the grandest hug he had ever given anyone.

"Good!" Ferraro interrupted. "I have noticed you both learn better together." He clasped their hands together. "You will do far greater things together than you would separately. Use that! Work hard, and I know you will both be exceptional."

Baccio and Trussi both nodded at the blacksmith. The awe of

becoming his apprentice made everything seem surreal. Trussi poked himself to make sure it wasn't a dream. "Good!" Ferraro cheered loudly, then smiled wide. "I expect to see you both early in the morning, ready to work all the harder." And with that, the boys started home. Just as the boys left the shop, Ferraro ran out to them.

"Wait! I almost forgot!" He offered his hand to Trussi and handed him some money. He did the same to Baccio. "Your wages from this last week. Keep up the good work." His smile still evident on his face, the boys shook Ferraro's hand again and thanked him gratefully. They continued home, the walk feeling unbelievably light, and it seemed like they had floated home. Once home, Trussi realized he was still clasping the money. He hadn't even looked at it to see how much was there.

They both entered the house, still in a daze. Trussi went to his room and put his earnings away in the secret place where he kept his money. He then went to the hearth and checked on the amount of stew they still had. There was enough left in the pot for both of them for dinner.

Trussi thought momentarily, realizing plenty of daylight was left. He knew of some abandoned apple trees, and the thought of roasted apples with dinner made his mouth water. The apple trees were farther than the pond, and walking there would take at least an hour.

"Hey, Baccio!" Trussi called out. Baccio poked his head out of his room. "Do you want to go pick some apples? I know where we can get some. It takes a while to walk there, but if we leave now, we should be home before dark. They taste wonderfully roasted over the fire, and we can have some tonight after supper. What do you think?"

Baccio smiled up at him. "That sounds great!"

Trussi smiled back. "Okay. You fetch some water. I'll get a sack to carry the apples home."

Trussi grabbed a linen sack. It wasn't big but would carry plenty of apples for them to enjoy. Before leaving, they drank their fill of water fresh from the pail. They then set out on the main road heading out of town. They followed it until they reached a fork in the road. Instead of choosing either direction, Trussi turned a sharp left and headed down a barely-visible trail.

His grandmother had shown him this path when he was very young, and Trussi was glad he remembered where it was. They continued following the trail for a long time, finding the walk simple and relaxed. After a while, they reached a large, old stump next to a small creek. From there, they changed directions and followed the stream. The further they traveled, the denser the trees and the brush became. Finally, they reached their destination.

Three apple trees grew right alongside the creek. They appeared slightly hidden among the surrounding trees and heavier vegetation. Bright red apples hung on their branches, ripe for the picking. Trussi smiled at the sight, remembering how sweet and juicy they were when he last came with his grandmother.

Trussi couldn't help himself. He reached up and plucked one of the apples. With a grin, he immediately took a large bite. Seeing this, Baccio didn't hesitate and did the same. The apples crunched with every bite, and they soon reached the cores. Baccio and Trussi ate several more apples, enjoying every crunchy bite. Once finished eating, they then started filling the small linen sack.

As they filled it, Baccio asked, "Trussi, how did you know about these apple trees? They're in the middle of nowhere."

Trussi smiled in remembrance of his precious grandmother. "My grandmother brought me here when I was young." He sighed, remembering her face when she first showed him this 'special' spot. "She said she came here to play with her sisters as a child. They planted these trees from the seeds of several apples they had eaten together. They returned to the same spot, watching the trees grow taller yearly, and ate the apples together when they bore fruit."

Baccio nodded his head in understanding. It didn't take long to fill the sack, and after a short rest, they headed back home. Trussi had often traveled to these trees alone, but Baccio's company made the trip seem considerably shorter. When they reached home, daylight was beginning to wane. It would be dark soon, so the boys built a fire in the hearth to warm the leftover stew. Trussi skewered several apples and roasted them over the fire as well.

They wolfed the stew and, as it didn't take long to roast the apples, Trussi and Baccio devoured them quickly. While eating the roasted apples, Trussi thought fondly of his beloved grandmother. He sighed, realizing he missed her more and more. Baccio yawned and bid Trussi goodnight before he headed to bed. Once Trussi was in bed, thoughts of the next day filled his mind. 'Tomorrow will be my first official day as the blacksmith's apprentice! Wait till I tell Giada!' And with that, he drifted off into a contented sleep.

CH. 6   PLANNING AHEAD

Trussi woke up in the morning and peaked outside. He sighed in relief to discover it was still dark out. He wanted to be on time on his first day as an official apprentice. Baccio was also getting up himself. Arriving to start the day, they discovered they would still be doing a great deal of observing. However, they both helped with small chores when asked, but much of the day remained the same. Trussi tried not to let his disappointment show as he had wanted to get his hands into the work.

Ferraro continued to explain more of what he was doing and why he was doing it. He spoke about why he heated iron a certain way and how cooling and reheating it in a certain way gave it strength but, if done incorrectly, made the metal brittle and weak. Several customers came, needing repairs done on varying equipment. Ferraro brought these items over to Trussi and Baccio, explaining how he intended to repair them. He also warned Trussi that if he restored these same items differently, they would be ruined rather than fixed.

Trussi made sure to soak up every explanation Ferraro gave. He recognized the invaluable information, knowing that much of this came from Ferraro's mistakes and errors. These lessons would save Trussi years of frustration as a blacksmith. Ferraro was training them more thoroughly now, and Trussi felt more confident in his new position. Baccio also appeared enthralled, keeping his eyes and ears open at all times.

As the workday ended, when they were leaving, Trussi desperately wanted to see Giada. He started walking toward the pub when Baccio turned and looked confused. Trussi sighed; he had not told the kid about Giada.

"Baccio, there is someone I want to go see before we head home." Baccio looked up at him, questioning. "Who's that? The widow?" Trussi shook his head 'no.' He then flushed at the cheeks thinking of Giada. "There's this girl, see, and her name is Giada-" Trussi swallowed hard. Why was it so hard to talk about her?

Baccio formed a mischievous smile and grinned from ear to ear. "Oh, there's a girl!!!!" His teasing tone didn't help, and Trussi found himself blushing deeper.

"Yes, there's a girl!" Trussi took a deep breath, trying to gain his composure. "Now that I'm the blacksmith's apprentice-"

"One of the blacksmith's apprentices." Baccio corrected.

Trussi rolled his eyes. "Yes, yes. Now that I am ONE of the blacksmith's apprentices, I can ask her parents' permission to court her." Trussi looked at Baccio, trying not to let his embarrassment show.

Baccio smiled at him, his teeth showing in his amusement. "So you're acting this way and haven't even started courting her yet?" He scoffed at Trussi, picking up his pace and running ahead.

"Hey, that's not funny!" Trussi fumed and chased after him. Baccio was fast for being a skinny little shrimp, and Trussi had difficulty catching up to him. Trussi may be strong, but he was too bulky to be fast on his feet. His irritation fizzled out as Baccio laughed and laughed. Trussi even started laughing at himself also. Finally, Trussi gave up on the chase with his breaths coming fast and deep. He didn't like giving up, but there was no way he could catch that kid. After taking a small break, he resumed the walk toward the pub.

Baccio eventually joined him on the walk again when he was sure the chase was over. They made it to the pub shortly and entered. Trussi looked for a small table for two and found one where Giada typically served. The boys sat down and waited to place their orders. Trussi was antsy to give Giada the news. He looked for Giada and beamed when she came into view. He watched her as she served the other tables, having not yet seen him. He saw her smile at the customers as she waited on them, showing off her dimples.

Trussi couldn't help but stare and continue to watch her. She was graceful in everything she did. Once Giada placed the food on the table, she winked at the customer and walked away. Trussi's stomach fell. 'She winked at that customer! She winked!?' He couldn't believe what he had just seen! Trussi's head became scrambled, and he couldn't think straight. He was so angry he couldn't think of what to say. His head felt like it had started to spin, and he was also beginning to feel nauseous.

He turned his head, surprised to find Giada standing beside him. She was looking at him, her eyes expecting some answer. 'Did she ask me a question?' It appeared so. He wasn't sure what she had asked him, so he said, "I didn't hear you. What did you say?" She leaned in and asked again in a monotone voice, "Did you get the apprenticeship?"

Trussi nodded his head, his anger still boiling up inside him. Giada squealed at his confirmation and nearly dropped her tray of drinks. She was completely unaware of the intense emotional stirrings inside him. Trussi grabbed her arm then. It wasn't hard, but it was substantial enough and brought her close.

He pointed to the customer she was just with. "Why did you wink at that customer? Are you interested in him? Is he trying to court you!?" Trussi tried not to sound so angry but was utterly unsuccessful.

Giada pulled her arm away and scoffed. "Certainly not. I wink at almost all of my customers...." She leaned close to his ear, saying, "I get better tips that way." Her voice was a matter-of-fact tone which helped offset Trussi's frustration.

'She winks at all of her customers.' he thought as his anger and confusion became apparent to those around him. Giada straightened her skirt out, then looked at Trussi, seeing the frustration still on his face.

"Oh, my goodness! You are JEALOUS!" She laughed out loud.

Trussi went from angry to embarrassed in just that moment. He turned his head away and looked at the floor. His head, still scrambled, wasn't sure what to say. 'Perhaps I should leave.' he thought hastily. His embarrassment now wholly replaced all of his anger. Just then, he felt a warm hand softly placed on his. He looked up to see Giada smiling at him.

She leaned close and said, "I am sorry I made you jealous. I have no interest in anyone else, and I am not being courted by anyone else either."

"Good," Trussi said gruffly. He grabbed her hand gently this time and pulled her even closer.

Giada leaned in closer, and Trussi could feel her breath on his cheek. "Don't be so grumpy, Trussi." She then laid a very light peck of a kiss on his cheek. Trussi shivered as goosebumps trailed down his neck, arms, and back. After winking at Trussi, she questioned, "Are you staying for dinner?"

Trussi nodded slowly, "What are you serving?" Trussi's words squeaked out. His voice barely worked correctly, and his arms and legs felt like they had become mush from her kiss.

Giada smiled. "We have fresh bread, porridge, potato soup, and boiled eggs."

Baccio spurted out, "I want potato soup!" Giada looked over at Baccio, seeing him for the first time. "Oh, and I want some bread too!" His smile was mischievous, and he looked like a young kid again.

Giada nodded to him and then looked at Trussi. "I'll have the same," he said.

Giada nodded, asking, "Anything to drink with that?" Her voice was smooth and relaxed.

"Just water." Trussi was glad he finally sounded normal. Giada smiled, winked again, and left the table. Trussi let out a big sigh and hung his head. Baccio cleared his throat, causing Trussi to look up. Baccio's mischievous smile was still present, causing Trussi to wince.

"What?" Trussi sighed again. His tone had turned monotone as he dreaded what Baccio would say.

"Oh, nothing..." Baccio said, still smiling at him.

Trussi snorted. "You're up to something. Spill it." Trussi tried to sound irritated, but most of his irritation had already dwindled.

"Nothing! Really!!" Baccio paused. "But if I ever act like this, please punch me." He made a mocking gesture of two people kissing.

Trussi rolled his eyes. "Yeah, yeah, enough." He waved his hand at Baccio. The kid stopped making the kissing sounds, but the goofy grin remained planted firmly on his dumb face.

It didn't take long for Giada to return with heaping bowls of potato soup. The bread was so fresh that it was still steaming as she presented it. She laid the items before them and smiled at Trussi. Immediately she returned to her other customers. Baccio and Trussi merrily started eating. The soup was so good! It had chunks of meat as well as carrots and celery. The bread was very soft, and Trussi couldn't remember the last time he had had bread this fresh. Giada returned several times as they ate, refilling their water cups.

After the meal, Baccio had a weird look on his face. "Is something wrong?" Trussi asked.

Baccio shook his head. He looked uncomfortable and antsy. After a moment, he finally admitted, "Okay, fine. I need to use the lavatory."

"Oh, no problem. We must pay the tab first, and then we can use the lavatory."

Baccio nodded, but then a panicked look appeared on his face. "I don't have any money!" he panicked as he patted his empty pockets.

Trussi sighed and placed a hand on his shoulder. "Calm yourself. I can pay the tab for both of us. You can pay me back when we get home." Baccio nodded his head as the relief was plain on his face. Trussi quickly paid the tab and asked for the key to the lavatory. He handed it to Baccio, who then ran off quickly.

Trussi felt some pressure on his left shoulder, causing him to turn. It was Giada, her smile widening as he turned towards her.

"So, who's the kid?" She nodded her head towards the lavatory.

"He's the orphan I told you about before." He loved the way Giada looked as she wrinkled her nose in confusion. "He's staying with me now as he has nowhere to go. The blacksmith decided to take us both on as apprentices, so we'll also work together."

Giada nodded in understanding. Trussi thought momentarily, then asked, "Now that I am an apprentice with a good trade, I want to ask your parents' permission to court you. Do you know a good time for me to do that? Should I seek them out tomorrow night?"

Giada shook her head. "Tomorrow is not good since we will be getting deliveries from out of town, and all of us will be very busy stocking the back of the kitchen." She paused a moment in thought. "What about this Sunday? After church, my parents are always in the most agreeable of moods. That would be the best time to approach them!"

"Then that's what I'll do." He clasped her hand gently and brought it to his lips. He touched the back of her hand with a light kiss and then leaned in close. "For you, I would do anything!" He meant every word. He really would do anything for her. Giada blushed deeply, taking her hand back slowly. She seemed to want to say something but nodded her head instead. Baccio returned just as Giada left to tend to her other customers. After some light teasing from Baccio, both boys headed home. Once they reached home, Baccio paid Trussi back the money from his dinner tab. It was still light out, and Trussi decided he had enough time to take some of the extra apples they had to the widow's house. Trussi asked Baccio if he wanted to join him, and the kid couldn't agree fast enough. Baccio picked out six apples to take with them. The walk went quickly, and they were at the widow's house in no time.

After dropping off the apples, they headed home, cleaned up, and were ready for bed. Just as Trussi went to wish Baccio a good night, Baccio looked up at him with a question. "Are we going to the pub tomorrow?"

Trussi nodded and said with a smile, "Yes." He wanted to see

Giada every chance he could before Sunday. Baccio's forehead furrowed as he thought. He didn't look too happy about returning to the pub. "Why? What's the problem? We have enough money to eat there every night this week with just enough left for the church tithe." Trussi tried to reassure him.

Baccio nodded his head but still didn't look too happy. "That's true, but that's it. After that, there is no more money until the blacksmith pays us again." Trussi nodded his head. He knew that but wasn't sure what Baccio's concern was.

"That means we have no money saved for anything. If either of us gets sick, then there is no money for a doctor or extra food for the days we don't work."

Trussi was starting to understand what he was saying. Baccio continued, "Plus, you want to court Giada, right?"

Trussi nodded his head again, thinking that was obvious. "Of course!"

"Then you'll need money for that. From the sound of things, Giada's parents want her well cared for. You need to be able to spend your money on the courtship to show her parents you can take care of her."

Wow. For Baccio being so young, he had things figured out. Trussi stood there in shock. He hadn't thought much about saving for the future. Trussi was so involved in what he wanted now that he hadn't thought about what he would need later. Trussi swallowed hard at this realization.

Baccio stepped forward. "I'm not saying I wouldn't return to the pub sometimes. Or that you shouldn't see Giada. What I am saying is that we should be smart with our money. We should always have some saved for later, for emergency purposes."

Baccio's eyes were intense, and he looked older at this moment. Those were not the eyes of a child but the eyes of a person who had seen terrible things beyond simple hunger. He was someone who had been through devastating events and had survived. Trussi placed his hand lightly on Baccio's shoulder.

"You are right. I need to be wise in how I spend my money. If Giada becomes my wife, I will need to be able to provide not only for myself but for her as well. I cannot give her the life she deserves if there is something she needs, and I am unprepared." Baccio looked relieved and placed his other hand around Trussi, embracing him in a quick hug. They bid each other good night and went to bed. Trussi lay in his bed, stressing over his conversation with Baccio. He wanted to see Giada every day. The thought of not seeing her turned his stomach sour, and, despite being very tired, his sleep was still restless.

Trussi woke in the morning with Baccio shaking his arm. "It's time to get up. We need to get going to work." Trussi stretched and wiped the sleep away from his eyes. He hadn't slept well, and waking up this early wasn't easy. Trussi was still groggy, and the walk felt much longer than usual. They made it on time and started their typical work day.

Once they finished the workday, while walking home, Baccio asked, "So, are we going to the pub tonight? If not, what do you want to do for dinner?"

Trussi stopped walking and paused. He still wanted to see Giada every chance he got. "I do want to see Giada. But, I also know I must save money, especially got courting her." He thought hard momentarily, and an idea soon popped into his head.

"How about this? I will go to the pub each night to see Giada. I won't stay long, and I won't order any food. I'll talk with her briefly to see and speak with her daily." Baccio nodded his head for Trussi to continue. "While I'm at the pub, you can go to the market and get what we need for dinner. We'll split the costs and meet at home and cook dinner together. This way, we'll both have plenty of money left over. What do you think?"

Baccio smiled and nodded his head again. "I like it. It's a good plan."

Relieved, Truss instructed Baccio, "Okay, good. First, we need to figure out what supplies you need for supper. I usually get some potatoes and other vegetables to make a stew. Sometimes I get meat from the butcher if he is there, but that can be costly..." Trussi rubbed his head in thought.

Baccio interjected, "So if the butcher is there today, do you want me to get some meat?" Baccio wanted clarification to make sure he got the right supplies.

Trussi thought for a moment. Finally, he shook his head. "No, I want to save as much money as possible. We'll go fishing if we need to get some meat sometime this week." Baccio agreed. Before parting ways, Trussi had one more tidbit to help save even more money. "Also, look for the stand in the market with the most crops. Sometimes they have extra vegetables that have started to go bad. If so, they'll usually sell them for a lower price. It doesn't taste as good but fills you up just the same, and it will cost less."

Baccio smiled. "I understand. I'll be sure to look around the market before purchasing any vegetables."

Trussi gave Baccio some money as they had agreed to split the cost of the food. And with that, they parted ways. Trussi watched Baccio leave, thinking how glad he was that Baccio was in his life now. From there, he headed over to the pub. Along the way, he saw some reddish-orange wildflowers. He picked one, thinking Giada might like it. Trussi continued his walk to the pub. Once at the pub, instead of taking a table like usual, he stood to the side, waiting for Giada's figure to fall into view. It didn't take long for him to spot her, and she spotted him shortly after.

She approached him, and Trussi found himself smiling. Once she reached him, she reached out her arms, and they hugged each other. Trussi held on, not wanting to let go. After a moment, she released her grip. Giada smiled up at Trussi then. "Sunday can't come fast enough," she said excitedly. Trussi nodded his head in agreement. Giada leaned back, looking to her left. "There is a table over there if you want to sit."

Trussi shook his head. "Sorry. I can't stay for dinner, but I just had to see you." A look of disappointment crossed her face.

Trussi remembered his flower and pulled it out, handing it to Giada. Although he hadn't known her for very long, he knew he wanted to spend the rest of his life with this girl. Giada sincerely smiled as she took the flower, placing it in her hair behind her left ear. It looked good with her complexion, and Trussi's heart fluttered at this site.

Trussi took her hand gently and placed a kiss on the back of it. "Not a day goes by where I don't want to see you."

They continued to speak to each other for several more minutes. Giada couldn't talk long and needed to return to her other customers. Trussi also knew he needed to return home to meet up with Baccio. Once Giada left his side, Trussi returned home. He found Baccio already there, cleaning the vegetables purchased from the market. The fire in the hearth was already roaring, so Trussi reviewed the vegetables Baccio had picked up. There were potatoes, as discussed, but he had also picked up some parsnips, broccoli, and cabbage.

Trussi groaned internally, as he was not fond of parsnips or cabbage. Then, Trussi noticed Baccio had also picked up some day-old bread. 'Not bad,' he thought. The kid did a good job negotiating a reasonable price for the food purchased. Soon, the smell of bubbling stew wafted up to their noses. It didn't smell very appetizing to Trussi, so he decided to review with Baccio which vegetables to obtain in the future.

Baccio interjected before Trussi could start, "Oh, just to let you know, I had a little money left after getting the food." He then handed Trussi half of the leftover money.

Trussi was surprised. "Wow, you did better than I usually do," Trussi admitted, happily taking the money. 'The kid's bargaining skills are better than I thought.'

Baccio smiled at this, then went back to tending the pot. "It doesn't smell as good as before," he said, looking disappointed.

"That's because you got different vegetables than I usually get," Trussi admitted.

Baccio nodded, asking, "So what vegetables do I need to get tomorrow?"

"Well, I usually get carrots instead of parsnips. And I don't often get cabbage. It depends on what is available at the market, but I sometimes get beans, artichoke when in season, potatoes, broccoli, and corn." Trussi listed off.

Baccio was looking at Trussi intently, paying close attention to the list. "Okay, I will do better tomorrow."

Trussi shook his head. "You did fine today. You even had money left over. Not bad for your first time bargaining at the market."

Baccio smiled at this, looking like a kid again.

Baccio then looked up at Trussi, adding, "It looks like we are getting low on firewood...."

Nodding his head, Trussi agreed. "Yes, we should chop some more for the week. I would also like to go fishing tomorrow. That will hopefully provide meat for a few days." Heading to the back of the house, they chopped enough wood for the week and carried it inside. Trussi then served the soup, and they started eating. It didn't taste terrible, but it wasn't delicious either. Still, it was hot food, and it still filled their bellies. Once done eating, they bid each other goodnight.

Trussi lay in his bed dreaming of Giada throughout that night.

CH. 7 COURTSHIP

The next few days went like before. The boys went to work, though much of their day required more task completion. Trussi stopped by the tavern each night after work and would talk with his special Giada for a bit. He wouldn't order food as he was earnest about saving money for courting her. As the week progressed, Baccio got better and better at picking vegetables for the nightly stew. Trussi also took him fishing twice, and they caught enough fish for the week. They had even caught several extra fish and took them to the widow's house.

By the time Saturday came around, they had a pretty good routine going. Neither seemed to argue or bicker about anything, and Baccio was a quick learner. Trussi never had to repeat himself on any of his instructions. That night, Trussi skipped going to the pub and went with Baccio to the market instead. He wanted to get a present for Giada. Something to show his romantic intentions and to show her parents he was a suitable suitor.

While Baccio looked around the market for dinner items, Trussi looked around for a gift. He found a stand selling trinkets, bobbles, and fabrics. He had some money saved specifically for this. He didn't want to spend everything he had, as he was more cautious with his money now. Looking around, he finally settled on purchasing some ribbons. They would be perfect for her! He had several different colors and patterns picked out, and the merchant wrapped them in pretty colored paper.

Excitement filled Trussi as he thought of what the next day would bring. As the boys walked home, Trussi saw some wildflowers growing along the edges of the fields. He decided he would pick some tomorrow on his way to church. He would have both ribbons and flowers to present to Giada. 'Pretty things for a pretty girl.'

His heart fluttered at this thought, and his stomach seemed slightly queasy as the thought of talking with Giada's parents entered his mind. He had to think about his words and ensure he approached them appropriately. Baccio noticed Trussi being severely quiet and cleared his throat loudly. Trussi shook his head. He hadn't realized he was so deep in thought.

"Yes, what's up?"

"You okay? You haven't said anything since we left the market." Baccio looked concerned.

Trussi nodded, "Yeah, I'm fine. I've just been thinking about what to say to Giada's parent's tomorrow. I haven't met them yet, and I need to make a good impression to ask permission to court their daughter."

Baccio seemed to understand. He was quiet for a moment and thought alongside Trussi. Finally, he said, "All you can do is be respectful. Think of them and treat them as you would a royal person. Being treated better than a peasant is enjoyable. If you do that, you'll likely gain favor with them."

Trussi thought about what he had said. It was excellent advice. But he needed to figure out how you would treat royalty. "So, how exactly would you treat someone who was a royal person with whom you wanted to gain favor?"

Baccio thought for a moment. "You have a gift for Giada, right?"

Trussi nodded his head. "Yes, I picked out some ribbons for her. And tomorrow, I also plan on picking some flowers for her on my way to church."

Baccio suggested, "Well, that's a good start. If I were you, I would also bring her parents a gift. One thing I know is everyone loves gifts."

Trussi had not thought of that. He didn't have anything to give to her parents and immediately became disheartened. It was too late to return to the market since all the stands were closed for the night. "That is an excellent idea, Baccio, but I don't know what I could give to her parents. I don't have anything else."

Baccio thought again, "How about the remaining apples? I think there are two left. We can always go to the apple trees tomorrow for more."

"Yes, that would be a good gift. There are no apple trees in town, so they are not likely to already have some. Though, two apples are not much. They would probably be a good gift for Giada's mother, but I still need something for her father." They both reached home just then.

"Let's think about it as we make supper," Baccio said as they entered.

Trussi paused and placed a hand on Baccio's shoulder. "Thank you, Baccio. You've been a big help. I hope I can help you the same way when the time comes." Baccio smiled in return. Once home, they both prepared the food for supper.

"Trussi, do you know what Giada's family crest is?" Baccio asked after he had finished dinner.

Trussi nodded, "Yes, her surname is Corvo, and her family crest is the Raven."

Baccio smiled, "Then that's what you should do for her father!" He exclaimed.

Trussi needed clarification. "I don't understand. What do you mean?"

"Can you carve different shapes from scraps of wood?" Baccio pointed to the pile of scrap pieces of wood and kindling.

Trussi thought about it and answered, "I don't know. I've honestly never tried to do that before."

Baccio suggested, "Then let's try it tonight. If you can carve a raven, it would show respect to their household and may bring favor with Giada's father."

Trussi raised his eyebrows. It was a spectacular idea if he could carve out a raven. "I'll try, but I don't know how it will turn out."

Baccio smirked and said, "Well, you'll never know if you don't try."

Trussi looked for a small piece of wood to carve. Once he found one he thought would work, Trussi used a small knife he owned but had rarely used. He sharpened it on a stone, then got started on the wood. Baccio had some experience doing this and helped Trussi through the project. The carving would be a little miniature, about the size of his palm. As he continued, the shape of the raven got more and more defined. After several hours, Trussi finally finished. 'Not bad!' he thought. It could have been better, but it was presentable and would make the perfect simple gift to Giada's father.

Baccio also approved. "It looks good, and if you wanted, you could blacken it by charring it with some of the cinders from the hearth." Baccio placed a glowing cinder on one of the kindling pieces. He removed it shortly after, showing the darkened burn mark on the wood.

Trussi wasn't sure if he should do this, but he decided the carving would look much better if it were dark, like a true raven. Deciding he would do as Baccio suggested, Trussi took a glowing cinder from the hearth. Baccio was helpful and instructed him to press the ember lightly and for not long. He only needed to press long enough to make a mark. He could set it on fire if he left it on too long. After he had placed several markings, Trussi felt like he got the hang of it.

He replaced the cinder in the hearth, picking out another fresh, glowing one. Repeating adding singe marks to the raven carving, it slowly darkened one spot at a time. Trussi liked how this gave the appearance of feathers on the raven. By the time he finished, it was late, and Baccio started yawning. Baccio looked at the finished raven, turning it side to side to evaluate the figure. "It looks excellent. Are you sure this is your first time at carving?" Trussi nodded and laughed. "I am very sure." He felt tired and yawned deeply as well. "It's getting late. We need to head to bed."

It was too warm to sleep under the covers, so Trussi lay on his blankets as he started thinking of Giada and how he would approach her parents. Before he could finalize anything, he drifted off to sleep.

The morning sun had barely seeped into Trussi's room as he awoke. He was tired but felt good about the day to come. As he got up, he could hear the sound of the church bells starting to ring off in the distance. Trussi went to check on the raven carving he had made. It looked like a real raven, and he was again pleased with himself. Trussi then used a linen sack to carry his gifts safely.

Both boys left shortly after, heading for church and Giada. Along the way to church, Trussi selected the prettiest flowers he could find. He gathered different ones and had a rainbow of colors compiled for his bouquet. He finished just as they made it to church. He gently placed the flowers in the sack with the other gifts and headed inside.

The preacher did his sermon, and the choir sang. Everything went as it usually should, except for Trussi. Trussi felt stressed on the inside. He couldn't even focus on what the preacher was saying. All he could think about was what he would say to Giada's parents. 'How am I going to approach them? Are my gifts good enough?' he kept thinking over and over.

Soon, everyone gathered for the tithing and prayers. Trussi took his place in line. He had nearly forgotten to bring money, but luckily Baccio had reminded him before they had left. After tithing, Trussi quickly went to the gathering area to look for Giada and her parents.

As Trussi entered, Baccio placed a hand on his shoulder. "You got this," Baccio reassured.

Trussi ran his hand nervously through his hair. He didn't feel like he 'had this.' He then spotted Giada and her parents. Taking a deep breath to calm himself, Trussi walked over towards them. Giada saw him approaching and smiled brightly. Once Trussi reached them, he nodded at Giada and looked up at her father. He was an older man with lines down his face and graying hair. His face was somewhat blank of expression and showed disinterest.

"Good morning, sir." Trussi tried to speak with confidence. He then looked towards Giada's mother saying "Ma'am." in greeting. They both nodded politely toward him. "It is a fine summer's morning." Trussi continued. "As such, I wanted to introduce myself. My name is Trussi. Trussi Greybear."

Her father reached out his hand, and Trussi shook it. "I am Antonio." Gesturing next to him, he continued, "This is my wife, Andrea." Andrea nodded toward Trussi, and he nodded politely back.

"And this is my daughter, Giada," Antonio said while gesturing towards his daughter.

Trussi smiled considerately. "It is good to meet you. However, I have met Giada several times before, down at the pub." Antonio raised his eyebrows. Trussi swallowed hard. "This is why I wanted to speak with you. I have romantic intentions for your daughter Giada. And, with your permission, I would like to court her."

Antonio looked at his daughter, then back at Trussi. "I hold my daughter in very high esteem. I will not allow just anyone to court her." Antonio paused momentarily, and Trussi felt a large lump forming in his stomach. "So, tell me, young man, what is your trade? Do you think you are worthy enough for my Giada?"

Trussi smiled, trying to portray confidence. "Sir, I am one of the blacksmith's apprentices. Once I complete my training, I can earn enough money to support myself, Giada, and a growing family. I have even brought gifts to show my honorable intentions."

He then opened his sack and pulled out the bouquet, and gently handed them to Giada. He then gave her the ribbons wrapped neatly in colored paper. She unwrapped them quickly and gave her father a very excited expression. Trussi then turned to Andrea and handed her his two apples, and a big grin formed on her face.

"Oh Antonio, Apples!! I do love apples!" She exclaimed.

Trussi then turned to Antonio and handed him the raven carving. The look on his face stayed plain as he took the carving. Trussi hoped it was enough to gain his favor. Antonio turned the raven from side to side, looking intently at it. Trussi couldn't tell if he liked it or not. After a moment, Trussi thought he almost saw the hint of a smile in the corner of Antonio's lips.

Antonio finally looked back at Trussi and placed the raven carving in his pocket. "These gifts are acceptable. And, as long as Giada wants this courtship...."

Giada looked at her father, "Oh yes!! Yes, father, I do want to be courted by Trussi!!"

Antonio nodded once, then looked back at Trussi. "Then I will permit you to court my Giada. However, if I feel your intentions are not honorable at any time, I will end the courtship without hesitation."

Giada squeaked, trying to contain her excitement. Her happiness showed on her face, and Trussi felt he would float away. He felt light all over, and his heart pounded hard. Trussi reached his hand out again to Antonio. Antonio reached out and shook his hand. "Thank you. Thank you from my heart. I will strive every moment to be worthy of your daughter." Trussi tried to keep his composure as his excitement made him eager to start the courtship. "When would be the best time to call on Giada?"

Antonio thought for a moment. "We are visiting her grandmother today. So, today won't work." He paused as he thought. "How about next Sunday? Giada works in the pub every evening, so Sundays are probably best."

Trussi nodded his head towards Antonio. "Yes, sir. That would be wonderful and thank you. I'll see you then on Sunday after service."

He then looked at Giada and repeated. "I will call on you next Sunday after church." He bowed slightly and reached out, clasping her hand and placing a small kiss on it. Giada smiled and blushed deeply. Trussi could now openly show affection towards her, even in front of her parents. He held his composure, but he was screaming with excitement inside.

Antonio shifted his feet. "Well, good day to you, Trussi. We need to get over to my mother's house to visit. She is expecting us."

"Good day to you, and blessings on your family." Trussi nodded his head. Giada giggled with her excitement. And with that, Giada and her parents left the gathering area. Trussi watched as his lovely Giada left, wishing he could go with her. He still felt so light. He was afraid that if he moved, he might genuinely float away.

Baccio's slap on his back woke Trussi from his near-trance. "You did good!" He said, smiling widely at him. "I told you the gifts would be a good idea."

Trussi reached out and placed one arm across the top of Baccio's shoulders, giving him a half-hug. "Yes, you did! And it worked perfectly." With that, both boys headed home.

Shortly after starting the walk, Baccio turned to Trussi. "So when are you going to call on her?"

Trussi sighed. "Not until next Sunday. She works every day except Sundays, so her father said I should call on her then."

Baccio nodded his head. "Well then, that's not much time for you to find another gift."

Trussi looked at Baccio, confused. "What do you mean?" He couldn't imagine trying to find or make gifts whenever he wanted to see Giada.

Baccio explained, "You should have a gift for your first courtship. You shouldn't need any additional gifts for her parents unless you feel you are falling out of favor with them. But, as your courtship with Giada continues, you'll need to bring her gifts occasionally."

Baccio looked at Trussi oddly then. Trussi looked confused and appeared to be in deep thought. "Trussi, you are older than me, and yet I know more about these matters? Haven't you ever courted anyone before? Or at least have seen someone courting?"

Trussi shook his head. "No, I have never been around anyone who was courting. I have also never courted anyone before Giada." Trussi took a deep breath, "My grandmother raised me after my mother died while giving birth to me. Though she taught me many things, she never discussed anything about courtship. And my father..."

Trussi paused for a moment as he rarely spoke of his father. "My father never spoke after my mother died, so I never learned such things from him. I never learned anything from him." Trussi turned away from Baccio. He looked towards the horizon, keeping his eyes unfocused as the memory of his father had always filled him with anger.

Baccio nodded his head slowly. "So, where is your father now? And your grandmother?"

Trussi stopped dead in his tracks. He hadn't wanted to speak of such sad things on such a joyous day. But, Baccio cared enough to ask, which was vital for him to know. "My father passed away several months ago from self-starvation. He had just given up. My grandmother..." Trussi's voice cracked. As he talked about her, his sadness over her loss filled him. He still missed her every day. "She passed away a few winters ago. She passed in her sleep from old age." Trussi could feel tears forming in the corners of his eyes. He fought them off as best he could.

Trussi continued walking, thinking about anything else in a feeble attempt to stave off the tears threatening to escape. "She was the strongest person I had ever met. She even had several sisters. Unfortunately, she lost her entire family, including her sisters, becoming an orphan herself."

Baccio listened intently. "How did she lose her family?"

CH. 8 LOVE AND LOSS

*** One Year Later***

The new day was ordinary, with both boys completing their daily tasks. Trussi had learned some basic sculpting techniques with the forge hammers over the last year and had started to master forming a variety of items. Items such as nails, simple candlestick holders, silverware, cowbells, horseshoes, and other everyday simple things.

But today was different. Trussi had been working on something exceptional. Something very close to his heart. Today, he would complete the ring he had been working on for a while. He was nearly done with the jewelry, as it only had a couple of fine details left to finish. He had been courting Giada every Sunday since he had gotten permission from her father. They walked together, had lunch with extended conversations, and even had one candle-lit dinner.

Usually, her mother or father would chaperone as they spent time together, so Trussi got to know her parents well over the last year. He had spent enough time with Giada to know, without question, wanted to spend the rest of his life with her. There was no doubt that he loved her with all his heart.

Trussi was ready to make it official and could envision her

wearing the ring he was making. Tomorrow was Sunday, and he would once again call on Giada to court her. Trussi already decided he would take her for lunch by the apple trees. But, this time, he would present her with a ring and ask her to marry him. Once Trussi completed his typical tasks, he started working on the final details of her ring. Over the last month, he had paid careful attention to the size of Giada's fingers. He wanted to be sure the ring fitted when she agreed to marry him. He finished placing the fine detail of an inscribed heart on the very top of the ring. Once he finished the heart, Trussi started polishing and smoothing all the edges. He reviewed her ring repeatedly, making minor adjustments until he finally felt it was perfect, just like his Giada.

During this last month, Trussi had spent much time hammering, heating, and shaping Giada's ring. This ring had been challenging to make, as he had to remake it three times. The first two rings cracked, and Ferraro stepped in after the second failure. He corrected Trussi on what he was doing wrong, and finally, the third ring formed perfectly.

Trussi took his ring to Ferraro for final inspection and approval. Ferraro eyed the ring, turning it around slowly. It was made out of iron, a less expensive and more common metal, as gold and silver were affordable for royalty or the wealthy. Though it was not a precious metal, the jewelry was stunning. It had a high shine with a near mirror-like finish and, to Ferraro, appeared perfect.

Returning the ring to Trussi, Ferraro commented, "You have done well. It will last a long time and is of excellent quality."

Trussi nodded his thanks, but Ferraro continued, "You are a fast learner, Trussi, and I'm impressed by how far you've come in such a short time." He came close to Trussi, placing a hand on his shoulder. "Starting Monday, I will show you how to make more complicated items. I'll also start having you repair broken equipment with me."

Trussi was surprised, "That would be amazing. Thank you!" He enthusiastically shook Ferraro's hand in appreciation.

"No need to thank me. Your hard work has earned it." He paused for a moment, pulling Trussi in close. "Now, you go see that pretty girl of yours. I want to know how it goes come Monday."

Trussi smiled back at him. "Of course!" To Trussi's surprise, Ferraro reached out and hugged him. Trussi had never hugged him before and was taken aback for a moment. The hug didn't last long, and Ferraro stepped back, sending him out and on his way.

Trussi and Baccio both went to the pub. Trussi went in and did his daily visit with Giada. He didn't stay long, just made some small talk before she returned to her customers. From there, the boys went to the market. Trussi went to see the baker, purchasing a small sack of flour and a bit of yeast, while Baccio went to buy vegetables. Once they finished, they headed home together. As dinner was cooking, Trussi looked towards Baccio. Over the last year, the kid had been well-fed and was no longer a skinny twig. The intensity of his chores had also increased, and he noticed the kid was bulking up nicely.

Trussi smiled to himself. Baccio would be fifteen this winter. It would be a short time before he would look at girls differently, and they would certainly look at him differently. Baccio saw Trussi looking at him. "What's with that weird look on your face?"

Trussi responded, "Oh, nothing. I was thinking about how much you have changed over this last year. You are no longer the skinny shrimp of a kid from when I first met you." He smiled at this thought.

Baccio rolled his eyes. "Yeah, yeah. I know what you were thinking about." He made a mocking motion of two people kissing and then laughed loudly.

Trussi smiled again. He was glad he had the kid in his life despite the occasional teasing he got from him. Trussi took in a deep breath and let out a long sigh. Despite this last year going so well, he was still unsure how tomorrow would go. "I don't know if I'm ready for this," Trussi mumbled.

Baccio scoffed. "Oh, come on! The ring you made for Giada is perfect. And besides that, you know she loves you. And her parents adore you. There is no way she'll say no."

Trussi shook his head. "I know she cares for me. But does she truly love me? Does she want to be with me for the rest of **her** life?" Trussi buried his face in his hands, his nerves getting the best of him.

Baccio placed a hand on his shoulder. "Of course, she will marry you. You have nothing to fret about."

Trussi nodded but still felt nervous about the day to come. He let out another long sigh again. Baccio stirred the pot and called over Trussi. "The stew is ready. Come and eat. You'll feel better with a full belly."

Trussi doubted that very much. Still, he filled a bowl and sat down to eat. After finishing his bowl, Trussi found his nerves did ease up a bit. He was feeling better after all. "Okay, you were right. Now that I'm full, I am less nervous about tomorrow."

Baccio smirked at him, saying, "Told you. Okay, so what's the plan for tomorrow?"

Trussi took a deep breath. "I will call on her late tomorrow. During the morning, I will gather everything we'll need for dinner. I also purchased flour at the market to make bread. When we court, I will take her down to the apple trees. When we arrive, I will tell her about my grandmother and why that place is so special. I will propose then, and we will make our first meal together as a couple."

Baccio nodded. "That's a good plan." He patted Trussi on the back. "You'll be fine. Just be sure to get lots of rest. I'll see you in the morning."

Trussi pulled out the ring he had made, looking it over for flaws one last time. It was still in perfect condition. He then went to his room to look for the small wooden box he had purchased at the market several months ago to present the ring in. It was a small wooden trinket box decorated with painted flowers. Trussi placed the engagement ring inside and wrapped it neatly in colored paper. He gently placed it in the middle of the table so it would be easy to find tomorrow.

It was still early enough, and Trussi had difficulty falling asleep. Finally, after a while, he got up and retrieved his book. It didn't matter the number of times he had read it. Trussi still enjoyed reading it every time. Pretty soon, his eyes became heavy. He put the book down next to his bed and finally drifted asleep.

The following day, church bells ringing off into the distance woke Trussi from his deep slumber. 'Today Giada and I will start our lives together,' he thought. Trussi left the ring at home as they went to church. He didn't want any chance of losing it. After church, he would still need to bake the bread and go fishing. There was still much to do before he would see Giada.

They made it to the church, and mass went like usual. Trussi had brought more money to offer today, hoping the extra prayers would help him later today. As he left for the gathering area, he was glad he received the additional blessings and felt more confident about the day. Once he saw Giada's parents, he approached them calmly but with an excited heart.

Trussi was greeted warmly by all. He turned politely to Antonio. "I would like to call on Giada today. I plan to take a stroll with her down the creek. I have a special place prepared where I want to make a meal with her later this afternoon."

Antonio nodded. "That would be fine. I will escort Giada this evening as Andrea is not feeling well."

Trussi then turned towards Giada. He reached out, lightly clasping her hand, kissing it tenderly. "Until tonight, sweet Giada." Giada squeezed his hand as if she did not want to let go. It wasn't until her father cleared his throat that she finally let go, and they parted ways.

Trussi headed home and fired up the brick oven. Mixing the ingredients, he made simple bread dough. While baking the bread, Trussi gathered the items he needed for the meal. The bread was ready shortly, and he pulled it out of the oven to cool. When he returned from fishing, it should be perfect for dinner. Trussi and Baccio left together, and It didn't take long before they were fishing, each in their favorite spot. The fish were biting well, and they headed home once they had caught enough fish.

When they reached home, Trussi wrapped the bread and placed it in a linen sack, along with the other ingredients for their meal. He then dressed in his best clothes, making sure he was well-groomed. Trussi double-checked his bag, making sure he remembered everything. The last thing he grabbed before leaving was the paper-wrapped trinket box he had placed on the center of his table in his room. Once that was secure in his pocket, he headed to the pub. He reached the pub shortly after and went to the right of the building.

Giada and her parents lived just above the pub. He walked up the stairs and knocked on the door. Antonio answered the door and smiled at him. "Trussi! Right on time." He embraced Trussi in a heartfelt hug, and Trussi hugged back.

"Hello, Trussi," Giada said. She had dressed in white with yellow trim, matching her hair's yellow ribbons. Trussi realized she was wearing the ribbons from his very first gift. Trussi couldn't help but smile. She was positively radiant.

"Hello, Giada. You look lovely."

He offered his elbow, taking her arm in his. They spoke back and forth as they walked, discussing pleasant stories and what they had experienced since last they courted. Trussi also apologetically informed Giada that their walk would take longer than average. He made sure to emphasize that the destination was very special to him. After a while, they finally reached the spot on the creek where the apple trees grew.

Giada gasped in awe as she saw all the ripe red apples hanging from the branches. Trussi explained about his grandmother, what she meant to him, and how the apple trees came to be. Giada and her father listened to every word intently. As Trussi finished his tale, he slowly bent down, getting on one knee.

Giada's face turned red before he could say a single word. Trussi pulled the paper-wrapped gift out of his pocket and handed it to her. She carefully and slowly unwrapped it, revealing the trinket box. "Oh, it is just lovely! Thank you so much, Trussi!" Giada smiled as she looked at the painted flower deportations on the box.

"You should... you should look inside." Trussi was almost unable to speak. Giada smiled again and opened the box. She gasped in surprise the moment she saw the contents.

"Beloved Giada, will you marry me?" She pulled out the ring, holding it in her palm, and displayed it to her father. She turned, looking directly at her father, seeing him slightly nod his head 'yes' in approval.

Giada turned back to Trussi. "Yes! Yes, I will marry you!"

Trussi embraced her, wrapping his arms around her in a great hug. Tears formed in his eyes. "Giada, darling, you have made me the happiest man alive." Trussi took the ring from Giada's hand and placed it on her finger. He was relieved to find that it was a perfect fit. Looking up, he saw she was already crying tears of joy.

Antonio came closer, and Giada stood up, lifting her hand to show her father the beautiful ring. Looking at the ring, he marveled at the craftsmanship. "What a lovely ring! It sparkles just like you." He said lovingly to his daughter. "We have much to tell your mother." Giada nodded her head.

Antonio turned towards Trussi. "I want you to come over next Sunday night to have dinner with us. There is much for all of us to plan."

Trussi nodded his head vigorously. "Yes, sir!"

He then laid out the large picnic cloth and all they would share for their meal. The meal went quickly, and Giada spoke about little things which delighted Trussi. Once they finished the meal, Trussi and Giada walked home slowly, hand-in-hand. It was just getting dark as Trussi left Giada at her doorstep. After a while, they bid each other farewell, and Trussi headed home.

Trussi found Baccio was already in bed sleeping when he got home. He felt disappointed having no one to share in his excitement. "I guess I'll have to wait for the morning," he mumbled with a smile.

Trussi went to bed then, his excitement spilling out and preventing sleep from finding him. He lay in his bed, thinking of Giada's face as she glowed wearing his ring. He eventually found rest at some point in the listless night.

Trussi was awakened by Baccio early in the morning. "Time to get up! We don't want to be late for work."

Trussi groaned. He was still fatigued and did not want to get up. Despite his body's objections, Trussi got up anyway. He could feel Baccio staring at him as they walked to the shop. Trussi looked over and gave him a smirk. Baccio laughed and slapped Trussi on the back hard.

"I knew it! I just knew she'd say yes!!"

Trussi nodded his head. "She said yes." His big goofy grin spread across his face. As they arrived at work, Ferraro looked at Trussi, his eyebrows raised, expecting an answer.

Trussi smirked again. "She said yes." He loved saying those words. Ferraro laughed loudly and slapped him in the same spot Baccio had. This time it had stung, and Trussi grimaced.

"Congratulations, my boy!" Ferraro shook his hand as he said this.

Without delay, they opened the shop with their usual routine and conducted business like any other day. The only difference was the giant grin on Trussi's face clinging all day. Trussi stopped by the pub after work to see Giada. As much as he would have liked to stay, he only chatted briefly. Both of them expressed their excitement at their new engagement.

Giada admitted she had been showing off her new ring all day long. After a short time, Trussi bid her a good night and left for the market with Baccio. That night, it didn't take long for Trussi to fall asleep as he was exhausted. He dreamed of Giada and what their wedding would hold.

Trussi woke up the following morning very early. He found he was still drained and yawned. He had a minor headache and felt groggy. He stretched a bit, hoping it would help. Trussi went to the window and checked outside, only to find it was still dark out, but with a tinge of orange like the sunrise, only somehow not, and there was no sign of light touching the horizon.

Trussi sighed as he realized he was up far too early. He went back to bed, annoyed but sleepy. It was then that he heard the sound of urgent knocking. It sounded like someone knocked on the front door. He groaned as he got up once again.

Just before reaching the front door, he heard the knocking happen again. This time it was louder and more frantic sounding. He went to the front door just as Baccio arrived, having been woken up also by the sound. Trussi did not know who would come knocking this time of night and carefully opened the door wide. The baker stood outside the door. He was covered in soot and gasping for breath. It was then that Trussi smelled it. Smoke!

The baker pointed towards the center of town. "Come quick! There is a huge fire down at the pub. We need everyone to help extinguish the fire before it spreads to more of the town!"

Trussi shouted his surprise and ran without thinking towards the pub as fast as he could. 'No! Not the pub!' He needed to find Giada and make sure she was okay. Giada had to be okay! SHE HAD TO BE!!

He ran towards the billowing black and white smoke rising from the town, seared by the flames below. As he approached the pub, Trussi saw flames rising above the other buildings. Once he finally reached the pub, as he sought with his eyes for Giada, he could see the entire building engulfed in bright orange and yellow flames. He didn't stop. He had only one goal, to get to Giada!

A crowd in front of the pub threw buckets of water against the flames, attempting to prevent the fire from spreading. Trussi reached the mass, gasping and nearly out of breath. He scanned the faces of the people there desperately looking for Giada and her parents but could not find her. He shouted out her name again and again in panic. Trussi still couldn't find her. He called out over the crowd's noise with no response, no Giada. Finally, he grabbed a person nearby by the arm.

"Where is Giada?! WHERE IS SHE?" he shouted at the startled woman.

She shook her head, crying, "I don't know! No one has come out!" Her hand pointed to the fire-consumed pub.

Trussi didn't think twice. He headed straight toward the flames. 'I will get her out. I will find her and get her OUT!!' He heard several men shouting behind him as he turned to enter the pub. He couldn't understand what they were saying. He only knew one thing! He had to reach Giada.

As he got near the building, Trussi felt the tug of someone pulling him back. Trussi shrugged this stranger off of him and continued pressing forward. More hands and more strangers pulled him back yet again. He fought them all. He had to get inside! He pushed people off of him left and right, fighting each one. Every step forward seemed to bring him two steps back. He was frustrated as he realized he was losing valuable time. He twisted hard then, giving one last colossal shove. Everyone fell away from him.

Trussi stepped one last time towards the pub when the entire building before him collapsed. He heard the sickening sound of wood rending and breaking, flames crackling, and glass shattering. Tall flames and thick black smoke billowed out where the pub once stood. Trussi screamed as he fell to his knees.

He continued to scream as tears flowed down his cheeks in dark soot-filled rivers.

Something snapped inside him, and he couldn't think straight. He got up and continued to try to get into the collapsed pub. He didn't care if he burned up with everything else. He had to get to Giada!! Again, more hands restrained him restrained from going forward. More hands and arms prevented him from reaching his goal. He howled in his frustration, making noises like a tormented animal. He vaguely heard shouts and screaming but could not discern any of it. He fought harder, oblivious of his strength, throwing strangers off him in large clusters. He pushed forward with everything he had. He was nearly there!!

Just a couple more steps!! Trussi could feel the fire's intense heat as sweat dripped down his face and neck. Just as he reached the very edge of the fire, he felt a hard and fast pain on the back of his head. And suddenly, all was black.

CH. 9 MOURNING

Trussi woke up with his head hurting tremendously. He discovered his entire body was stiff and sore as he tried to move. He groaned as he sat up, increasing the pain radiating from the back of his head. Looking around, Trussi realized he didn't recognize his surroundings. He was in a bed, but it wasn't his bed. He was in a room that wasn't in his house. Pushing the blanket aside, he groaned deeply again. Just as he was doing this, he remembered what had happened. The fire!! "Giada!!" He shouted. He remembered he had to find her. "GIADA!!" he called out again. Trussi finally tried to get up to run out of the room but only managed to get a few feeble steps.

The door swung open. Ferraro stood before him with Baccio close behind. Ferraro rushed over to Trussi, placing his hand on his shoulder. "It's okay, Trussi. Let's get you back to bed. You need to rest."

"No, I have to find Giada. I have to make sure she is alright!" Trussi's voice sounded weak and exhausted.

"No Trussi." Ferraro's voice was stern and commanding. "You need to go back to bed and rest."

"But, Giada..."

"...is gone, Trussi." Ferraro interrupted. He swallowed hard, with tears forming in the corners of his eyes. "I am sorry, but she is gone." His face was solemn and intense, looking Trussi in the eyes.

Trussi opened his mouth. He wanted to scream. He tried to

scream out the pain radiating within him. But no noise came out, and pain filled him from the inside. Tears flooded his eyes and streamed down his face.

Ferraro supported Trussi with one arm and partially carried him back to the bed. Trussi sat there momentarily, thinking this had to be a bad dream. A horrible dream! Baccio came into view just then, his eyes looking tired and sad. He reached out, wrapping his arms around Trussi. Trussi looked desperately into his eyes. "No!..... It can't be true!...... Giada..." Trussi's voice trailed off, carrying his horrible pain and desperation.

"It's true, Trussi. I'm sorry, but Giada is gone." Baccio also had tears streaming down his face. His eyes were red as if he had been crying most of the night.

Trussi fell back on the bed, sobbing. His hands shook as the gravity of the loss of his Giada continued sinking in. He would never see her beautiful face ever again. He would never hold, touch, or kiss her ever again.

He wailed and moaned between the sobbing and convulsive gasps. Ferraro left the room while Baccio stayed by his side. Baccio decided that even if he could not comfort Trussi, he could ensure he would not be alone. Finally, Trussi had cried himself back to sleep. After many hours, he awoke, finding his sadness was even more profound. His head was still pounding, and his mouth was drier than sandpaper.

Baccio was ready for him with a tall cup of water. Trussi gulped the water down, but the moment he swallowed the last drop, he resumed his heart-breaking sobbing. He continued mourning for hours until he passed out yet again. The day progressed this way, with Trussi waking, sobbing and wailing, and passing out again. Ferraro and Baccio rotated shifts of who stayed in the room, so Trussi was not alone. Between passing out and crying, Trussi willingly drank water. He was offered food but refused to eat so much as a bite.

By the end of the day, everyone was exhausted. Trussi no longer had the voice to wail and moan, but tears remained streaming down his face as he woke. He also didn't speak or acknowledge

Ferraro or Baccio. The night seemed to blur into the day, and the day blurred into the night again. The sound of the church bells finally woke Trussi up from his stupor.

'Is it truly Sunday morning?' he thought. He knew this meant he had been lying there mourning for six days! Trussi sat up slowly, still sore. His pillow and sheets were still wet from his constant sobbing. The church bells rang again in the distance, and listening to them gave him a tiny fragment of peace. He sat there for a while, quiet, listening to the bell's soothing ringing. After a short time, he got up. The room was empty save for himself, and he still wasn't sure where he was. Ambling, he left the unfamiliar room.

The house was unfamiliar to him as well. It was modest but comfortable and clean. He wandered down the hall, passing by another empty room until he entered the main living area. Trussi saw the hearth had a fire and a big pot with stew boiling in the center. Baccio was stirring the soup, and when he looked up, he saw Trussi approaching. Baccio's eyebrows raised as he saw him.

"You're up."

Trussi nodded in Baccio's direction, giving him the first acknowledgment he'd seen since being in this house.

"How are you feeling?" Baccio asked, looking concerned.

Trussi sighed. "I'm feeling tired and sore." Trussi held his hand up, pointing towards the pot. "And, if I'm being honest, I'm pretty hungry also."

Baccio smiled and nodded. "I'm glad to hear that. You haven't eaten anything since you got here." He turned around, grabbed a bowl from the counter, and filled it with stew from the pot.

"I don't know where 'here' is." Trussi's stomach growled at him as Baccio handed him the bowl.

Baccio replied, "Oh, this is Ferraro's house. He brought you here when, well, right after you were knocked out." Baccio didn't look at him when he said that, avoiding direct eye contact.

Trussi's eyes narrowed. He had almost forgotten someone had hit him in the back of the head. He felt behind his head then.

The goose egg from the impact was nearly gone, but his head was still very sore. Trussi's stomach growled at him again. He knew he should eat something soon. Trussi sighed and gulped down the stew, barely tasting it. Instead of feeling satisfied, his sadness seemed to intensify, and he could feel tears forming in the corners of his eyes once again. Pushing past the tears and pain, he continued consuming the stew until the bowl was empty.

"So, where's Ferraro?"

Baccio shrugged. "He left for church just a moment ago. I didn't want you to be alone, so I stayed." Baccio looked at Trussi, his eyes showing relief. "I'm quite glad to see you up and talking now. I didn't want to lose you as well."

Trussi nodded his head absentmindedly. The loss of Giada entered his thoughts again, causing pain to swell up inside him. He was on the brink of sobbing again when he felt warm arms wrapping around him. Baccio was hugging him. The hug brought Trussi slightly out of his painful daze, and he hugged Baccio back. Baccio was here for him, just like a brother would be. He was in Ferraro's house and being cared for like a good father would care for his son.

Trussi remembered his father for a moment with morbid sadness. 'These two people have done more for me in the last week than my father had done for me in my entire life.' Tears welled up in his eyes again. He was so grateful to have Ferraro and Baccio in his life.

"Thank you for being here for me. I don't think I could have made it without you." Baccio already had tears in his eyes. He nodded, buried his face against Trussi's shoulder, hugging him tighter. The hug lasted a while, both of them quietly holding each other. The last of the church bells stopped ringing in the distance, and Trussi could hear the soft chirps of birds singing in the morning radiance.

Trussi finally let Baccio go, wiping his eyes. The bowl was still in his hand, and he held it up. "Is there more?" Baccio gently smiled and refilled his bowl. When Trussi finished, a sigh left his lips as the ache in his heart overpowered him. He sank to the floor, sitting where he had just stood. Baccio came over, sitting next to him.

Reaching up, he placed a hand on Trussi's shoulder. "I know it hurts. But you'll get through this. It will get easier."

Trussi looked up at him, tears already streaking down his cheeks. "I can't imagine my life without her, Baccio. How do I get through this? How?"

Baccio whispered, "You get through this as everyone does, one day at a time."

Trussi looked down, burying his face in his hands. His eyes ached from all his crying, yet more tears poured out. Baccio continued to sit next to him as he wept, quietly keeping him company. It took a while for Trussi to gain his composure and stop crying. He was able to get up, with Baccio's help, and walk back to the room where he had awakened. He lay in the bed, silently weeping until he passed out again.

The sound of soft, muffled voices in the distance woke Trussi from his restless slumber. He got out of bed and headed back to the main living area. Baccio and Ferraro were quietly talking with each other. They immediately stopped as Trussi entered. Trussi tried to speak, but his throat was so dry that he croaked. He tried to swallow but only made some dry, gurgling sounds. Baccio appeared in front of him with yet another tall cup of water.

Trussi took it, drinking it down fast. After the third refill, he continued drinking the cool water, finally quenching his thirst. He looked over at Ferraro, nodding towards him.

"Baccio tells me this is your home. I want to thank you for letting me stay here through this...." Trussi paused for a moment, pushing back tears. "...difficult time."

Ferraro shook his head. "No need to thank me. You are always welcome in my home." His eyes held sadness, and he looked just as tired as Baccio. "So, how are you feeling, Trussi?"

Trussi shook his head. "Not well. My heart aches, my whole body hurts, and everything feels hopeless. I don't know how to go on without Giada."

Ferraro got close to Trussi, placing both hands on his shoulders. "Believe me. I know how much pain you are experiencing. And I know it feels like this is the end of the world. But you will get through this."

Trussi shook his head. "I don't know how I'll get through this." He could feel tears forming in his eyes again. He pushed them back as hard as he could.

Ferraro's grip on his shoulders tightened, and Trussi saw the pain on Ferraro's face. "I had a girl once, too. We had only been married briefly, and it was the happiest time of my life." Ferraro looked down at the floor. His eyebrows furrowed at the painful memory. "She used to pick flowers every morning. And one day, while picking flowers, she was stung by a bee. She had never been stung before, but she had a reaction to the sting and died that very day." He looked up at Trussi, his eyes intense but sad. "I know the pain you feel, Trussi. And that pain will kill you if you let it. Don't let it kill you. You can get through this."

Trussi looked at him, surprised. He had never known anything about Ferraro's past. He slowly nodded at Ferraro as his intensely personal story sank in.

Ferraro continued, "I don't want you to give up, Trussi. And I know Giada wouldn't want you to give up either." Ferraro released Trussi's shoulders and walked over to the pot of stew. "Now then, let's eat some food. Lord knows you certainly could use a meal."

Shaking his head, Trussi held up his hands. "No, no, thank you. I've already had two bowls earlier."

Ferraro's eyes narrowed. "In the last six days, that's all you've had. You will need more if you are to gain back your strength. You've already lost a great deal of muscle. Look how baggy your clothes are!"

Trussi looked himself over for the first time. Ferraro was right. As he felt around his stomach and arms, Trussi felt smaller than he had been. Ferraro handed him a heaping bowl of stew.

"Eat. Then you'll need a bath. You stink."

Trussi realized he had not cleaned himself since arriving at Ferraro's house. He reluctantly smelled himself. Yep, Ferraro was right. He smelled rancid.

"Don't worry about it," Ferraro said, waving a hand. "Baccio already has the bathtub filled. The water is warming as we speak and will be ready shortly."

Trussi looked at him, confused. "The water is warming? How is that possible?"

Ferraro smiled, looking pleased with himself. "The water is being heated uniquely. You'll have to take a bath if you want to know." Trussi had never had a warm bath before. He had only ever cleaned himself in the creek or used buckets of water from the well. The thought of a warm bath helped him to focus on something other than his pain, and he contemplated how anyone would construct such a feat.

Trussi started eating the stew slowly. His stomach seemed glad to get the food, but the ache in his heart turned sour. If he finished the bowl, he would chance retching up the nourishment his body desperately needed. He put the half-empty bowl down. "So where is this warm bath?"

Baccio smiled, "Follow me."

Trussi followed him down the hall. They entered a small room with a large brass bathtub in the center. The tub was golden colored and raised on four legs. Under the tub was a small indented pit filled with hot coals. Trussi placed his hand in the tub of water and raised his eyebrows in surprise. The water was warm. Very warm!

Baccio handed him a towel, and Trussi didn't wait. He undressed immediately and slowly eased himself into the warm bath. It was hot, and it felt soooo good. Once fully relaxed in the tub, he leaned back, allowing his entire body to relish in the soothing warmth. He could feel every single muscle slowly relaxing. Even his nausea disappeared. By far, this was the most relaxed Trussi had been in a very long time. Probably the most comfortable he had ever been in his entire life!

Trussi let out a sigh of relief. 'Ferraro is a genius!' he thought.

He decided then and there that he would need to build a bath like this one. Trussi sat in the bathwater for quite some time, profoundly relaxing and enjoying the warmth. He found himself fighting to stay awake as the heat from the water soaked deep into his muscles, soothing every ache in his body. He wasn't sure how much time had passed, but when Ferraro knocked on the door, Trussi's hands and feet were wrinkled.

"How are you doing in there, Trussi? Everything alright?"

Trussi let out a relaxed sigh. "Yes. Everything is fine. This bathtub of yours is a marvelous piece of craftsmanship. I thought it would be nice to have one at my home."

Ferraro chuckled. "Okay, Trussi. If you need anything, holler."

Trussi heard Ferraro's footsteps leave, and he leaned back into the warm tub. He didn't want to get out of the bath but knew it was probably late. He found a small cleansing cloth nearby and used it to scrub the stink and sweat off of himself. Once he was sure that he no longer reeked, he reluctantly got out of the tub, drying himself with the towel Baccio had left.

He looked around for his clothes but discovered they were not present. Confused, he checked the room again and still did not find them. Trussi left the room with the towel wrapped around his waist. Looking out the window, he saw it was just getting dark outside. Baccio and Ferraro were in the main living area together. Trussi could see that the baker was also with them and conversing.

Trussi cleared his throat, saying, "I'm sorry to interrupt, but I seem to have misplaced my clothes."

Baccio shook his head. "I took your clothes. They held as much stink as you did. Your clothes are now clean and are outside drying on the line."

Trussi became instantly irritated. "You should have consulted with me first. I do not wish to wear a towel for the remainder of the night, nor do I wish to wear wet clothes!" Baccio put both hands with his palms up in the air. Ferraro laughed at Trussi and cut in before he could say more.

"Baccio has already brought a clean change of clothes. They

should be ready for you on the bed."

Trussi huffed a bit, his irritation fizzling out fast. "Good." He should have known better; Baccio was far more considerate than he gave him credit.

Trussi turned around, returning to the room he had been sleeping in, and found a clean shirt and pants on the bed. Thinking about the bath as he got dressed distracted him from thinking about Giada. The warm water had been the only physical comfort he had felt in the last six days.

Once finished, Trussi went back out to the main area again. The baker had been the one to knock on his door, alerting him about the fire, so Trussi was anxious to speak with him. There was one huge question on his mind he wanted to ask. The baker looked tired to Trussi as he approached. They greeted each other and shook hands.

"Good to see you, Trussi. I'm glad to see you are feeling better."

Trussi nodded. "Thank you, sir. And I'm glad to see you also. I have some questions about the fire."

The baker shrugged his shoulders. "I don't know if I have all the answers, but you are welcome to ask."

"Please, sir, can you tell me, do you know how the fire got started?"

The baker shook his head as he looked at Trussi with pity. "I am sorry, but I do not know what started the fire. No one does. Once the building collapsed, there was nothing left intact to be able to figure out what started it. I know there are several different ideas people have discussed. Some think a disgruntled customer may have started the fire, as about nine or ten others perished in the inferno. Some think a kitchen fire probably caused it, but no one truly knows."

Trussi nodded his head. He would not get the answers that he wanted from the baker. "Thank you, anyway." He turned away, trying not to cry. It wouldn't have changed anything, even if he had discovered how the fire had started. Giada was gone, and nothing was going to bring her back.

"Thank you for coming. I appreciate it." Ferraro said to the baker.

They shook hands again, and the baker left. "Trussi, you look like you are feeling better. Come, have dinner with us." Ferraro gestured for Trussi to sit. He was given a plate with grilled meat, potatoes, and a large piece of bread. "The baker was kind enough to bring us some supper."

'This bread looked like day-old leftover bread,' Trussi thought. Still, it was food, and it wasn't moldy, so Trussi sat down and joined in the meal. He didn't eat much, but he did feel slightly better with each bite. It felt nice to share a meal, each making a light conversation about how dry the bread was or how the weather was that day. Despite being tired, Trussi joined in the discussions. He started asking questions about the bathtub and how Ferraro emptied it after each use. Trussi couldn't imagine using a bucket to scoop and dump it.

Ferraro explained that a small pipe connected to the bottom of the tub to a drain valve. When you turn the valve one way, the tub remains filled. Turn the valve the other way, and the tub water drains out the pipe. He also explained that he had the pipeline drained out to the backyard and into some planter boxes where he grew herbs and vegetables. Watering his planter boxes this way saved him time and effort in retrieving additional buckets of water.

Trussi was fascinated! Ferraro was brilliant in coming up with such a contraption. They spoke about it for some time, and Ferraro described how the idea had come to him. It was a good distraction for Trussi, and he was glad to focus on something besides his pain.

Once it was very dark outside, they each went to bed. As Trussi was alone, sitting on top of the bed, all he could think about was Giada. He felt so incomplete without her. He wasn't sobbing or crying like before but felt empty and hollow. Despite these unnerving feelings, falling asleep didn't take much effort.

The soft sounds of two people talking woke Trussi up early in the morning. He found his body was far less sore and achy than previously. 'That warm bath sure has miraculous effects,' he thought. Walking out to the main living area, he found Baccio alone.

"Where's Ferraro? I thought I heard him?"

Baccio answered, "He just left for the shop."

Trussi's eyes narrowed. "Then we need to head over to the shop too."

Baccio shook his head. "No, Ferraro wants us to stay. He says you need more rest...."

Trussi interrupted, "All I have been doing is 'resting.' And I have had enough rest." Trussi headed for the front door. Baccio trailed behind him, looking concerned.

"Are you sure we should be doing this? Ferraro was adamant."

Trussi insisted, "Yes, I am sure!" His irritation showed as he walked faster towards the shop. They reached work just as Ferraro arrived. He looked surprised upon seeing them there.

"Baccio, I said to stay home today. I can take care of the shop."

Trussi didn't let him finish talking, either. "I am not staying home today. I have come to work."

Ferraro shook his head. "No, Trussi, you need to go back and rest..."

"I HAVE HAD ENOUGH REST!" Trussi had never shouted at Ferraro before, and Ferraro raised his eyebrows in surprise but said nothing. Trussi shook his head, calming himself. "I am sorry for shouting. But I cannot stay in bed any longer. All I do is think of Giada and how much I want to be with her. If I stay in bed anymore, I'll lose my mind."

Ferraro ran a hand through his hair as he thought, carefully considering Trussi's words. "Please, let me stay in the shop. I need to work."

Ferraro sighed. He opened his mouth to say something, then stopped. "Fine, you can stay and work today. But I am in charge! If I think you need to leave, you had better leave." His eyes were intense, and his tone resolved. Trussi nodded in agreement. Ferraro nodded, too, and turned around. They all entered together and opened the shop.

CH. 10 HIJACKED PLAN

Seven years later

"**G**oodbye, dear!" called out Baccio's wife. Baccio turned around, embracing his wife in a passionate hug and long kiss. Trussi rolled his eyes and groaned at the site. He tapped his foot impatiently as they continued their morning farewell. The two embraced each other like this every day, and Trussi could barely stand the sight of it.

In these last several years, Baccio had had no trouble finding himself a girl to fall in love with and marry. They had courted for a while, and the two were married last year. The girl immediately moved in with Baccio even though Baccio still lived in Trussi's house. The girl's belly was large and round, with their first baby expected to be born in a few months.

Baccio finally finished his farewell and headed out the door with Trussi. Once they arrived at work, they entered and opened the shop, starting the day with their everyday routine. Ferraro was absent in the mornings, as that was now the norm. Once Trussi and Baccio had learned considerably more and could both operate the forge efficiently, Ferraro started sleeping in. With him gone in the mornings, this would leave the two nearly half the day to themselves.

After he had lost Giada, Trussi concentrated and poured himself into his work. Pounding red hot metal with his hammer allowed a minor release of his anger and frustration over time. Eventually, he found some small measure of peace. While Trussi relished the freedom he got from the physical work of his job, he also enjoyed working on problem-solving tasks. His favorite thing to work on was locks. He could easily fashion intricate keys to specialty locks and unjam or unlatch any lock brought to him. This specialty skill gained him many customers despite his irritable disposition.

Customers came, and Trussi bartered with them just like Ferraro would. He didn't budge very much on his prices as Ferraro did, but he was always fair and never cheated a customer. Trussi knew he was grouchy and didn't care. He wasn't out to make friends or indulge someone else's feelings.

No, he had plans of his own. Trussi had decided long ago to leave this small town and have his own adventure. Trussi had read his book The Golden Mountain so much he nearly had the entire thing memorized. Trussi had known for a long time that he didn't want to stay in this town. He already decided that when he did finally leave, he would use the book descriptions to find a golden mountain of his own.

He often spoke to Baccio and Ferraro about this dream, but neither took him seriously. 'Little do they know, I have been saving up money for this grand adventure of mine,' he thought to himself while a hint of a smile crept across his lips. Trussi had also stocked up his supplies and was finally ready to leave this year. Once Ferraro paid him for the week, he would let them know his departure plans for tomorrow morning.

Trussi continued to work hard, ensuring everything was ready so Baccio could continue working tomorrow without him. Trussi had his mind on his big adventure and was mentally reviewing everything, ensuring he had thought of everything.

He didn't even notice when Ferraro had arrived midday.

Finally, the end of the day had arrived, and the shop was ready to close. As they were completing their closing tasks, Ferraro noticed something about Trussi.

"You're being quiet today." Ferraro pointed out, nodding his head towards Trussi.

"He's been like that all day. Barely any words come out unless he's talking with a customer." Baccio stated as he looked over at Trussi. His eyes were mischievous, and he looked like he was up to something. "I can't think of a day when you didn't groan or complain about something I've done or haven't done or about one of the customer's unrealistic expectations."

Trussi sighed. "Yes, I know I've been quiet today. I have something on my mind."

"What exactly has been on your mind?" Baccio smiled at Trussi. His tone was playful and hinting at something.

"Why are you talking like that?" Trussi looked up at Baccio, annoyed.

Baccio's grin widened. "Oh, no reason. Just wondering what was on your mind. Or, should I ask, who is on your mind?"

Trussi rolled his eyes. "Oh, not this again. Look. I am not interested in any girls that come by batting their lashes at me or giggling like geese!" He turned around in a huff, trying to concentrate on closing up.

Baccio laughed. "Okay, okay. I just thought that girl from yesterday had maybe caught your eye. She had spoken with you for quite a while."

Trussi remembered that girl. She was nice enough and pretty enough to be likable. But no one ever came close to touching his heart, not like Giada. Trussi sighed.

"Yes, that girl. As I recall, that girl talked about how her father and mother were both sick, and the family barely got by." Trussi shook his head. "It's funny. I lowered my price for her, only to see her later that day at the market with her parents. They didn't look ill. She just wanted a better price for the items she wanted."

Baccio and Ferraro both scoffed. Baccio wouldn't let it go and came to the girl's defense. "And so what if she did! She did seem to like talking and flirting with you. Not that you would give her or anyone else a chance! My word, Trussi! How long are you going to wait? You are a fine catch, and any girl would be glad to..."

"I don't WANT any girl." Trussi was more than irritated. Now he was getting mad. "I don't know why you keep bringing this up. There was only ever one girl for me. I am not interested in anyone else, and I will NEVER be interested in anyone else!"

Trussi threw his hands up in the air in frustration and walked away. Trussi knew he would do or say something he would regret later if he didn't stop immediately.

"Look, Trussi. I'm sorry. I promise I won't bring it up again." Baccio felt bad for egging him.

"No, you won't." Trussi looked at him, his eyes intense as his irritation still boiling inside him.

Trussi sighed again, releasing some of his annoyance. Looking around one last time, Trussi decided there was nothing left to do in the shop. Ferraro paid both Baccio and Trussi and bid them goodnight. Trussi suddenly cleared his throat, getting the attention of Ferraro and Baccio. He had been dreading this conversation but knew there was no avoiding it.

"Before heading home, I must tell both of you something."

Ferraro looked at him questioningly but did not interrupt.

"I just want to let you both know that today was my last day in the shop."

Both Ferraro and Baccio appeared to be surprised and visibly upset.

"You can't be serious, Trussi!" Baccio nearly shouted. He couldn't understand why Trussi wouldn't be returning to the shop. "Look, if it's about me teasing you, I promised I wouldn't repeat it. I..."

Trussi cut him off. "It isn't that, Baccio." Trussi paused. This discussion was more challenging than he thought it would be. "I am not returning because I am leaving town. As I have discussed many times, I am leaving to find my adventure."

Baccio scoffed at him again. "Oh, not this again! You're going to leave because of that silly book of yours! You think you'll find treasure and become rich!?!"

Trussi smiled. "I have no delusions about becoming rich. I am leaving for the adventure! I want to see the world beyond our little village here. If I were to find treasure, yes, that would be nice. If I don't ever find any treasure, then so be it! I don't care! But I am leaving." He gulped as a lump started to form in his throat. He would miss Baccio, truly miss him. Telling him that he was leaving was difficult. "I am leaving tomorrow. I know the carnival will leave in the morning, and I will leave with them."

The carnival came from the land of the giants. It had been coming into town each year around the same time for the last fifty or so years. These giant people tower over everyone else in town and are five to six feet tall. Besides the colossal delivery man that comes into town delivering supplies once a month, this was the only person who came in from out of town.

The carnival brought exotic foods and spices for trade, as well as exotic fabrics and other rare supplies. Trussi's favorite thing about them was the storyteller! The carnival travels around, going from land to land and town to town, gathering stories and telling of great adventures. He had listened to these stories since childhood, fueling his desire to go on an adventure of his own.

Both Ferraro and Baccio looked at Trussi, shocked. Neither said anything, though both appeared to have much to say. Trussi continued before either of them could start arguing further.

"I am going to the market to buy the final necessary supplies. Baccio, I'll see you at home in a little while." With that, Trussi turned around and headed towards the market. He didn't need much as he was prepared well for tomorrow's departure. Trussi knew he needed to bring food that would last longer than just a few days, such as jerky and hard tack.

He had already stocked up on seeds for various vegetables and spices, as he would need to start a garden wherever he might settle. While at the market, Trussi also picked up an extra pair of travel shoes and thick travel blankets. He also purchased two small leather water flasks, making sure he only chose those of superb craftsmanship. From there, he headed home.

Baccio's wife was already preparing dinner when he returned home. Trussi gave her the items he had picked up for dinner, and she happily took them, adding the ingredients to the boiling pot. Trussi took his travel bag out of his room and shuffled through his supplies.

He added his ax and pickaxe to the contents. He also filled his two flasks with fresh water from the well in the backyard. He reviewed all his content again and was satisfied with what he had. Baccio's wife hollered that dinner was ready, and Trussi ate at the dining area. Baccio was there, though Trussi had not heard him come home. They ate dinner together awkwardly, not saying much and avoiding eye contact.

When finished, Baccio had had enough. "Trussi, I don't understand why you are so determined to leave. The life we have here is fine. We want for nothing!"

Trussi shook his head. "It's not that. I can't describe it, but I have wanted to leave town ever since I could remember. Before I had ever met Giada." Saying her name out loud caused Trussi to cringe. He rarely spoke of her, though he thought of her often. "It feels like this is my destiny, Baccio. I am supposed to leave. I am supposed to do this."

"No, you're not." Baccio shook his head, tears forming in his eyes.

A loud knocking at the front door interrupted him from continuing. Baccio turned away, wiping his eyes. He opened the front door, finding Ferraro and the local Doctor with his son standing outside. Baccio invited them inside, though he was perplexed about why they were there. They entered, and they all greeted each other politely, shaking hands.

'If they think they can talk me out of this, they have another thing coming!' Trussi thought, ready for a fight.

Ferraro smiled awkwardly and shifted his feet nervously. "Well, I guess I better explain why we are here." Baccio and Trussi both nodded. Ferraro sighed, looking over to Trussi. "Trussi, I know you are dead set on leaving, and nothing I can say or do will change your mind, right? Right." Ferraro smiled just then devilishly. "Well then, I guess I am coming with you. I am all packed and ready to go."

Trussi was completely surprised and nearly fell over. Ferraro had never mentioned or indicated he wanted to join him on his adventure. 'What?!' Trussi thought. He had planned to go on this trip alone. He never intended for anyone to join him!

The Doctor interrupted Trussi's thoughts. "Well, it's not just Ferraro. We are coming too." He gestured to himself and his son, who appeared to be no more than thirteen or fourteen years of age.

"Okay, this is ridiculous. There is no way I am going on this trip with three other people!! Everyone needs to slow down! Ferraro, can you please explain to me what is happening? Why do you, and why do they think you are all coming on this journey with me?" Trussi huffed as he tried to tether his growing frustration.

Ferraro looked at Trussi. "I know I never told you I planned to come with you. I thought you would sneak out and leave without me if I ever did tell you. I have lived in this village my entire life and have never done anything adventurous." Ferraro sighed. His face looked pained as he spoke.

"When I lost my wife, the life and the family we both wanted all died with her. I couldn't bear to even look at another girl after losing her. Heck, I've been a blacksmith for more than forty years, and if it weren't for you and Baccio, I would probably still be alone."

Trussi tried to object, but Ferraro continued regardless, "I want an adventure just as much as you do, and finding treasure with you would be amazing also. I am not here to convince you to stay or tell you this is a terrible idea. I have already decided to come with you, which is final." Trussi stood there, dumbfounded. He couldn't respond to anything Ferraro had said.

Ferraro turned and gestured over to the Doctor. "This is my good friend, Doctor Dottori, and this is his son, Remo. I invited them to come with us as well." Remo looked at Trussi with a big grin filling his face. Trussi looked at them, positively astounded.

Dottori looked at his son, then looked at Trussi. "I know you don't know us, but we want to accompany you on this journey."

That was it. Trussi had enough. He shook his head. "Listen, Doctor Dottori, I..."

Dottori interrupted, "Doc. Please. Just call me Doc. I never did like the way Dottori sounded."

Trussi gritted his teeth, and his hands clenched in frustration. "Fine, Doc. I don't think you should accompany me on my travels. You are not at all ready for how hard this journey will be!

I have been preparing for this adventure for years!"

Doc shook his head. "Ferraro told me about how he wanted to go on this adventure several years ago. It interested me, as I have never felt much at home in this town." Doc sighed. "You see, my parents were impoverished and struggled every day. As I became older, I was determined to make my life better. Luckily, I was able to become a doctor's apprentice. After many years, I eventually became a doctor. I was even blessed enough to find someone to love. I lost her just as she gave me my only son." Doc looked down at Remo.

"I couldn't save her during the complicated childbirth. Since then, I've seen fewer patients as they are going to other doctors. This village is slowly shunning me, and I have known I would need to move on for some time. When Ferraro invited me to come on this adventure, I couldn't be more thrilled to come. My son and I are ready, and we know it won't be an easy journey."

Trussi opened his mouth to object. Ferraro held his hand up. "I know, Trussi, but as I have said, we have already packed and are ready to go."

"What do you mean you are ready to go?!?" Baccio looked just as shocked as Trussi.

Ferraro walked up to Baccio, placing a hand on his shoulder. "I have taught you everything you need to know. I am getting too old for such hard work, and you can run the shop yourself." Baccio shook his head. He appeared just as frustrated as Trussi.

"That is why I am retiring and giving you my shop," Ferraro interjected.

Baccio looked up at him. His eyes opened wide, and he was nearly on the brink of tears. "You can't leave me too... With Trussi leaving, what will I do, who will...."

Ferraro smiled at him. "You will have your wife and newborn child to care for soon. Believe me. You will not be lonely." Ferraro paused briefly, pulling a key out of his right pocket. "And this is the key to my house. It is bigger than this one." Ferraro placed the key in Baccio's hand. "And now it is yours. Consider this my farewell gift to you and your wife." He leaned in, whispering in Baccio's ear, "I hope she likes my bathtub."

With tears in his eyes, Baccio chuckled at this last comment. "Thank you. I can't thank you enough for everything." Baccio embraced Ferraro letting the tears fall down his cheeks.

"Keep an eye on Trussi, okay? Don't let him do anything stupid."

Ferraro chucked and hugged Baccio back. "I'll keep as close a watch as I can."

Trussi was still trying to convince them to reconsider. "Look, I appreciate you wanting to leave this village and go on an adventure. That doesn't mean you can hijack mine! I..."

Ferraro cut him off again. "And what are you going to do if someone robbed you? Have you ever thought of that? Look, you know that it is dangerous to travel alone. There are wild wolves and groups of robbers out there. If you travel by yourself, then you are vulnerable. But, if we travel as a group, we would be stronger together and safer."

Trussi couldn't argue with the logic that Ferraro had presented. He had never considered robbers or personally facing dangerous animals such as wild wolves. He opened his mouth to refute, and again he couldn't think of anything to say.

Finally, after a moment of thought, he shook his head. "Fine. I can't stop you from joining me on my journey. But don't think for a moment that I won't hesitate to leave you if you fall behind or hinder me in any way! And, and..." Trussi paused to take a deep breath, attempting to calm himself. "...and if you can't handle that, don't bother coming! I'll be leaving early in the morning. If you aren't up and ready to go, then you get left behind!" Trussi turned and walked away, too frustrated to discuss anything any further.

Both Doc and Ferraro bid Baccio good night and left. From there, Baccio went to the back of the house, following where Trussi had fled. He found Trussi attempting to relieve some of his frustration by kicking the well in the back of the house. Trussi wanted to punch something but knew better than to do something stupid and hurt himself. Trussi saw Baccio come out and turned away from him, embarrassed.

"Don't start. Just don't." He kicked the well again.

Baccio folded his arms with a slight smirk forming. "I don't know what the well did to you to deserve your wrath, but I'd go easy if you ever want it to draw water again." The humor was unexpected, and Trussi couldn't help but laugh. It was just like Baccio to find the humor in something so frustrating. Trussi stopped kicking the well and turned back.

They stood there for a moment, not saying anything to each other.

Trussi finally broke the silence. "You know the most challenging thing right now is leaving you. I would have left long ago if it weren't for you."

Baccio gave a half smile. He didn't want to see Trussi leave either. "Well, as long as you promise me you'll return, I can't object to you leaving."

Trussi nodded his head slowly. "Of course, I'll come back. I gotta show off all the treasure I find." He tried to make a joke, but it didn't seem to lighten the mood nor reassure Baccio. He sighed loudly. "Okay, fine. I promise that when I have had enough adventure, I will come back." Baccio looked down at the ground nodding his head.

Trussi walked over to Baccio and placed both hands on top of Baccio's shoulders. "I will return. I swear that to you."

Baccio gave a quick hug. "You had better." They let go, and both headed back inside the house. Trussi would need plenty of sleep tonight if he were to leave on time.

CH. 11   FAMILY SECRETS

Trussi awoke the following day. It was early enough that it was still completely dark outside. He quickly and quietly gathered his travel items and slowly crept out of the house. Baccio woke up quickly and caught him right outside the front door. There was not much to say between them, so Baccio wished him farewell. He then gave Trussi the last three apples they had.

"I know you only have travel food, so take these. You may want something fresh after a long day of traveling." Baccio's words were said quickly, and direct eye contact was avoided.

Trussi nodded his thanks and left. He knew everyone at the carnival would already be packing to head toward the larger cities. Trussi also knew the walk there required passing by Ferraro's house.

As he walked, Trussi sighed as he noticed Ferraro, Doc, and Remo standing outside, looking ready to go. Trussi stifled a groan and walked over to greet them. They looked tired, but their bags appeared packed, all dressed in plain travel clothes. Once Trussi acknowledged them, he turned, heading again for the carnival.

Once they reached where the carnival had been, only two caravans remained. They were already starting to leave, so Trussi picked up the pace to keep sight of them. The others, he decided, would have to keep up or be left behind. When they got to the town's border, Trussi turned, looking back at his hometown one last time.

'Yes,' he thought, 'I am doing this for real!' A deep but sad smile formed, and Trussi continued walking briskly.

As they walked, the sun rose slowly, pouring its daily warmth. After a while, they reached the fork in the road. Trussi glanced to his left, looking down the trail which led to the apple trees his grandmother and her sisters had planted. He was grateful then that Baccio had given him some apples to take with him and looked forward to eating them later. The caravan turned right, and Trussi continued to follow.

Trussi had never come this way and could feel his renewed excitement. For many hours he traveled this new unknown road to where? It didn't matter. He was finally on his adventure. Trussi glanced back once in a while to check on the others. They kept up and made no complaints about the pace of the journey. Finally, near the end of the day, they came upon another crossroads. At this point, the caravan stopped. Another group of processions came from a different direction, and the two joined into a sizeable single troupe.

Once combined, everyone started setting up tents and making campfires. 'They must be stopping for the night. 'Thank goodness!' Trussi thought. Everyone sighed in relief and started to set up their separate camp. Once finished, Trussi didn't hesitate to pull out one of his fresh ripe apples. He smiled as he was about to take a big bite when he felt eyes watching him. He looked to his left to see Remo staring at him with big wide hungry eyes.

The kid wasn't just staring at him. He was licking his lips. Trussi huffed and turned away. 'This is my apple!' He put the apple to his lips and stopped. Trussi looked back at Remo. He wasn't staring at him anymore but looking at the ground with a pitiful and sad expression. "Man, I am such a sap." he groaned to himself. Walking over, he gave his precious apple to Remo.

Remo smiled big and quickly took a big bite out of the apple. Trussi paused, waiting for a 'thank you' or something along those lines. But the kid kept right on eating the apple. "You know, it's rude when you don't say 'thank you' when someone gives you something." Trussi sounded more irritated than he meant to. The kid stopped eating mid-bite and looked up at Trussi.

Doc stepped in, "Sorry, Trussi. I thought you knew. Remo is mute." Trussi looked over at Remo, who smiled and nodded his head. He then went back to happily munching away at the apple. "He can hear you and understand what you say. He just can't speak. I would have said something sooner, but I thought you already knew."

Trussi shook his head. "I didn't know."

He poked the kid on the shoulder, and Remo looked up at him again. "I'm sorry I became irritated at you for not talking. That won't happen again." Trussi walked away, returning to the group's center where Ferraro had lighted a small campfire to help keep them warm for the night.

Trussi sat down right when Ferraro came over. "Listen, Trussi. We need to go into one of the caravans and see if we can buy extra blankets."

Trussi groaned loudly this time. "Why do you need me? You should have packed more blankets!"

Ferraro kept his voice low. "It's not for me! It's for Doc and Remo. They packed some lite blankets, but you and I know it won't be enough when the cold sets it. They will need more to stay warm and survive."

"This is why I wanted to come alone on this journey!" After a brief pause, he questioned, "Why do you need me? You invited them. You can go buy the blankets yourself." Trussi looked at him, feeling even more frustrated.

Ferraro narrowed his eyes and lowered his voice. "I need you to come with me. None of us should be alone around strangers, especially when you have money to spend."

Trussi let out a big sigh. "Fine, but I'm not the one who is buying the blankets. You are."

Ferraro nodded in agreement and told Doc they were going to get supplies. Before going into the caravans, Trussi grabbed his two remaining apples from his bag and immediately bit into one. He then grabbed his travel pack, taking nearly all his supplies.

Ferraro looked confused. "Why are you bringing your entire travel pack?"

Trussi softly smiled. "Well, you said there were robbers in the big world. If there are, I'm not taking any chances."

Ferraro rolled his eyes. He knew that tone of Trussi's irritated sarcasm. Heading over, they wandered around, going from camp to camp. Few peddlers were open as most had set up camp for the night. Finally, Ferraro spotted the one with some blankets for sale and other travel goods.

Ferraro approached the peddler, and Trussi stayed close, wanting to avoid the conversation. Trussi finished his apple and tossed the pit into a nearby bush. He glanced back at Ferraro, who was still negotiating. He started pacing slowly at first. His impatience was getting the best of him.

He stopped pacing suddenly when he heard the distinct sound of someone crying. Looking around, Trussi didn't see anyone right away. He glanced around again and saw an older woman in a camp behind the peddler whom Ferraro was still negotiating. The old lady was crying softly, and Trussi couldn't help but walk closer to see the problem.

She was alone while sitting next to a small campfire. A small travel sleep sack and an old, worn walking cane were beside her. She buried her face in her hands, and she was weeping. As Trussi got closer, the old lady looked up from her hands. He could see the tears still streaming down her face.

"Ma'am, I came over to see what was wrong. What has happened to make you cry so much?"

Her shaky hand gestured to her sleep sack. "I travel alone as most of my family is no longer living. I am traveling to visit my grandchildren, but the journey is long, and I am quite tired." Her lip quivered as she spoke. Trussi looked her up and down. She was short for a giant and was very thin and frail looking.

"I had brought food for my journey, but thieves have stolen it along with the little money I had. More tears streamed down her face. "I don't think I have the strength to continue. I won't be able to see my children or grandchildren again." She looked at the ground, again placing her face in her hands.

Except for her height, the old lady reminded Trussi of his grandmother. A bun held her long silver hair, and she had deep wrinkles around her eyes from years of smiling. Trussi instantly felt tremendous compassion for the lady and didn't hesitate to help her. He dug into his travel pack, pulling out some of the dried meat he had packed and the third apple he had yet to eat.

"Ma'am, I don't know how far you have to go, but you may have some of my food to help get you there." She looked up from her hands with surprise at his kindness showing on her face. She reached out, slowly taking the food from his hands. She immediately started eating the jerky. Trussi dug into his right pocket as she ate, pulling out a little of his money.

"Take this too. You can refill your food supplies when the caravan reaches the next town." He handed her the money as she finished the last of the jerky.

"You are so kind! Thank you so much, sir. Please. Come sit with me." She patted the spot next to her on the ground.

Trussi didn't want to stay but sat down anyway. He wasn't quite sure why, but he was drawn to this silver-haired lady. She turned and was about to bite the apple but stopped and looked at it. She turned it side to side, examining the apple intensely.

"This is an exceptional apple. Where did you get it from?" she asked.

Trussi was hesitant but answered anyway. "I picked it from the apple trees my grandmother and her sisters had planted many years ago." Trussi was shocked at himself. He couldn't stop himself from being so open and honest with her.

"Hmmmmmm. Very interesting."

She turned the apple again, then looked at Trussi. Her eyes had changed from sadness to something else that looked like hope. "Was your grandmother's name Vecchia?"

Trussi felt a wave of shock flow through him, and the hair on his arms stood on end! He could barely speak above a whisper. "Yes. Yes, that was her name. How did you know? Did you know her?"

The old lady smiled, but it was a sad smile. "Yes, I knew her. She was my sister, and we planted those trees together." She looked at the apple one last time, then slowly took a small bite.

Trussi looked at her, unable to move. 'This is my grandmother's sister, which means she is my great aunt! Grandmother had told me that she had lost her entire family. How was this possible?'

She continued eating her apple until nothing was left. "Thank you. That was so special to me. I never thought I would have another apple from those trees again." She turned to him, looking him up and down. "I see you have some questions. You may ask them." She paused for a moment and smiled. "My name is Strega, by the way."

Trussi swallowed. "My grandmother told me she had lost her entire family but never told me what happened. How is this possible?"

Strega sighed. "It's unfortunate. My older sister and I were born normal-sized, and the youngest, Vecchia, was very small like you."

Trussi nodded his head. He hadn't considered himself or others from his town as being small. He had always considered himself normal-sized, and the others outside the village were giants.

"No, we are not giants." Strega continued. The hairs on Trussi's arms stood on end again, and he couldn't move. "Your town is full of small people called dwarves. Everywhere else, every town and every village is full of normal-sized people like me. There are a few villages high up in the mountains with true giants, and they are anywhere from fifteen to twenty feet tall."

Trussi's mouth hung open. In all his dreams, he had never imagined anyone being that tall! Strega nodded her head. "Yes, being born a dwarf meant Vecchia would live a hard life, which was an embarrassment to our mother. Our mother took her to your town when she was twelve and abandoned her there."

Trussi was appalled. He wanted to shout out how terrible that was, that it was wrong for her mother to do that! But still, he remained motionless.

"We lived in the town next to your village, and my older sister and I would sneak out, meeting up with her to play together. We planted those apple trees together, returning to watch them grow year after year.

"When we were older, our mother found out. She said we would become proper ladies and avoid anything associated with a lower status. So, she moved us far away, and I never saw Vecchia again." Strega looked over at Trussi. "I see her in you, though." She smiled, placing a hand on his. Where she touched him, Trussi could feel it tingling.

"I want to thank you for your kindness, Trussi. Very few are left in this world who would have helped an old beggar woman like me." Trussi couldn't remember telling her his name.

She smiled again, winked at him, and looked him straight in the eyes. "I would like to reward you, Trussi, for your kindness. Please, hand me your pickaxe." Trussi nodded. He put his travel pack down, took out the pickaxe, and then handed it to Strega as if following an order. She took it and started stroking the top, front to back, systematically. While she did this, she chanted something under her breath in a language Trussi could not understand.

After a moment, she handed Trussi back his pickaxe. "I have enchanted your pickaxe. It will only work for you, so if another uses it, the enchantment will not work for them."

Trussi swallowed hard and asked, "What kind of enchantment?" Strega leaned in and whispered to him, "No matter where you use this or what it strikes, it will bring you a fortune." She smiled again, reaching up and touching Trussi's cheek. "You look so much like Vecchia. I miss her as much as you do."

Trussi had never been told that before about his resemblance. It felt odd coming from someone he barely knew. He looked down at his pickaxe. It looked the same as before, but now it felt different. He couldn't pinpoint what it was that felt different.

"Oh, before you go, Trussi, I have one more thing I need to tell you." Trussi looked back up at Strega. "I want you to beware of the queen." "The queen?" Trussi needed clarification.

Strega nodded. "Yes, she is as cruel as she is beautiful. She is the ruler of this land. She is also a terrible witch, dealing in dark magic to get what she wants."

Trussi's eyebrows rose. He had heard of the queen in some of the carnival tales. But they were mostly about her beauty, not her evil witchcraft.

"Yes, Trussi, she is a witch. She married the king, who already had a lovely child, a young princess. He passed away shortly after they were married, and the queen has ruled this land ever since. She is obsessed with her physical beauty. She is so obsessed that if anyone rivals her, she kills them." Strega shook her head. "I fear for the little princess trapped in her keep."

Trussi started feeling antsy. He knew Ferraro would be looking for him by now, and he cleared his throat, wanting to excuse himself.

"BEWARE THE QUEEN!" Her voice was nearly a shriek. "My sister Regina no longer shows kindness to anyone. Beware, and stay far away from her."

Trussi gasped. "Wait, wait. The queen is your other sister?"

Strega nodded her head slowly. "Yes." She sighed deeply, looking solemn once again.

"Shortly after we moved, she had a noble suitor, which would have brought our status up. Mother was so proud. But a fairer maiden won the affections of her desired suitor. After my older sister's failed courtship attempt, our mother started teaching us magic. I learned white magic, magic that helps others. My older sister, however, delved into black magic used only by dark witches. She used that dark magic to make herself the fairest in the land, gaining many suitors wherever she went.

"This black magic she uses also keeps her looking young no matter how many years pass. But her dark magic has a bitter price. Piece by piece, with every dark spell she cast, she slowly became less and less my sister and turned more into a monster."

Trussi shook his head. There was so much to take in here. "So, you are sister to the queen and sister to my grandmother. The queen, the eldest of all of you, looks young instead of old. And, she is renowned for being the fairest in the land?"

Strega nodded her head again. "Steer clear of her, Trussi. Or else, I fear the worst for you." She paused momentarily, then stood up and pointed to the caravan where Ferraro was shopping. "I do believe Ferraro is looking for you."

Trussi looked behind him, seeing Ferraro looking around while holding some thick travel blankets. Trussi stood up, waved his hand, and Ferraro spotted him. Trussi looked back at Strega, only to find she was no longer there. Not only that, but everything around her was gone. The fire, the sleeping bag, even her footprints were gone! It was as if she had never been there.

Ferraro jolted him out of his dazed state by slapping him on the back. "There you are! I was worried you had left me alone. Come! Let's get back to the others."

One look at Trussi's face and Ferraro knew something was wrong. "What's the matter, Trussi? You look like you've seen a ghost!"

Trussi looked at him, his eyes still open wide. "I... I am not sure. Well, that is, I may have just seen a ghost. I'm not quite sure...." He realized that he still held his pickaxe. Trussi shook his head. Did all of that happen?

Ferraro's eyes narrowed, looking Trussi up and down. "Trussi, let's get back to the others. Then you can tell me what happened." Trussi nodded, and they left, heading back to Doc and Remo. They hurried over and reached their camp quickly. Ferraro handed off the blankets he had acquired and then turned to Trussi.

"Okay. Tell me everything that happened."

Trussi sucked in a deep breath. He wasn't sure how to start, as there was so much to say. He first told Ferraro about his grandmother taking him to the apple trees and that she had told him she had lost her family, though she never told him how. He then told Ferraro about seeing an elderly lady crying and everything that happened afterward. Trussi did leave out the part where Strega enchanted his pickaxe as he needed to figure out how Ferraro, a retired blacksmith, would react.

Once Trussi was finished, Ferraro had an earnest look on his face. He let out a big sigh. "That is an incredible tale, Trussi. If I didn't know you and knew you weren't a liar, I'd think you'd have just made it all up." He shook his head.

"I don't think she was a ghost. You wouldn't have been able to feel her hand if she was." Pausing momentarily, he continued, "I have also heard terrible tales of the queen. Some say she is so beautiful that a glance into her eyes will cause you to fall instantly in love with her, as if by magic. Others tell of her cruelty. However, this is the first I have heard of witchcraft." He paused again, thinking to himself.

After a long moment, Ferraro finally spoke. It is wise if we try to avoid trouble as much as possible. We should steer clear of the queen and her castle." Trussi nodded in agreement.

Trussi was still restless, tossing and turning most of the night. So much turmoil was going through his head. 'Is my grandmother the queen's sister? Was she a witch too?' and other thoughts sifted through his mind until sleep finally found him.

CH. 12 THE SEVEN

Ferraro quietly awakened Trussi. "Trussi, wake up. There's a problem," he whispered and shook Trussi awake carefully. Trussi groaned and felt as if he hadn't slept at all. He blinked several times before he realized what Ferraro had said and sat up quickly.

"What's the problem?" Trussi looked around, seeing it was still dark. On the horizon, it was just starting to get light.

"Come with me but be quiet!" Ferraro's voice was barely above a whisper.

Trussi got up just as Ferraro put out the fire. The other two were already quickly packing up all their gear carefully. Trussi packed quickly and quietly, and they were all ready to move. Ferraro led the way between several of the other campsites.

Everyone else seemed to be sleeping, and Trussi didn't understand the issue or why Ferraro was hurrying them along. They were about halfway through the camps when Ferraro stopped.

"Right here." Ferraro pointed to the dark side of a particular group. "This was one of the groups that joined in from one of the other roads."

Trussi looked closer. Several prominent people were sleeping around a campfire and a smaller group of three off on the side. The three were huddled together and covered under sleep blankets. They seemed smaller than the others around them. 'Perhaps they are children?' Trussi thought. It was then that

Trussi noticed the chain on each of their ankles. They were chained together.

Ferraro and Trussi approached these three very slowly and quietly. "I am back and brought help," Ferraro whispered to the chained group.

The sleeping covers quietly slipped off and revealed three dwarves. They were not children at all but prisoners! Ferraro pointed to the chain on their ankles. "Trussi. Do you think you can pick that lock? I have already tried and was not successful."

Trussi looked at the lock briefly and nodded. It was a simple lock, and he could easily unlatch it with the right tools. Luckily he had brought some of his lock-picking gear with him. As Trussi dug in his bag to get his lock pick, one of the people sleeping by the campfire groaned and started to shift around.

"You better work fast, Trussi. I think these people are going to be getting up soon." Ferraro's voice, though urgent, was calm and quiet.

Trussi found the tools he was searching for and immediately picked the lock. It didn't take long for him to get it open, and they unshackled themselves quickly. Everyone followed Ferraro, going through the camps until they reached the center of the crossroads.

"Which way should we go?" Doc asked.

"Let me think." Ferraro's face creased with worry.

"So, you woke me up to liberate these three, and now you tell me there is no plan!" Trussi was instantly irritated. How could Ferraro be so reckless!! If the caravan were to awaken soon, they could all end up shackled together. He sighed, weighing their options in concentration. Luckily an idea came quickly.

"Okay, fine, this is what we do. We came from the south following one caravan while the other came from the west. Given this, our options are either north or east." Pausing a moment, he considered both options. "I think our best option is to head north."

Ferraro shook his head. "The caravan was going to head north this morning. If we go that way, we'll get caught. Perhaps we should go back south. We can hide these three in our town and..." Trussi cut him off. "I am not going back! If anyone from the caravans looks for escaped dwarves, our town will be the first place they'll look. They'll also look in the towns they were passing through, in case these three had escaped and sought refuge there. So, they will probably search the towns from the south and west just in case they flee there. The last place they will look for them, or us, is in the north. So that is where we must go."

Ferraro thought, the furrows in his forehead relaxing a bit. "I hope you're right, Trussi. We'll go north if you think it's the best path."

Trussi pointed down to the ground. "This is a dirt road. We need to walk alongside it, not on it, so they won't be able to follow our footprints." Ferrari and Doc nodded. They all started quietly but quickly walking alongside the north road. They wanted to get as much distance between them and the caravan as possible. The sun was already rising, and they had to hurry.

They stopped for rest and ate about midday without seeing the caravan behind them. Once everyone had a bite to eat and some water to drink, Trussi decided he needed some answers.

"Okay, Ferraro, you need to explain yourself. What is going on? Why were these three chained up like that?" Trussi gestured to the three newcomers.

Ferraro nodded and explained, "I couldn't sleep last night, so I went for a walk. I thought if I could clear my head, I would sleep better. It was then that I came across these three. They were enslaved, chained up, and forced to be performers and laborers."

"It's true." One of the three orphans spoke up for the first time. "I've been with the carnival since I was five years old. These two were only four when they started. Since they first brought us here, we have had to complete laborious tasks and perform as clowns. If we refused, then they would beat us and deny us food. We tried to escape many times but were never successful. Eventually, they put a chain on us so we couldn't flee. When Ferraro found us last night, he said he could help us! And he did, with you!"

Trussi looked at the other two. One seemed a bit sheepish, hiding behind the one that was talking. The third had sneezed several times and rubbed his nose.

Trussi sighed deeply. "So, how old are you now? And what are your names?"

"I am twenty-one years old now, and these two are twenty. We, uh, we were never given any names. They always called out 'Hey you!' or 'Dwarf!' to get our attention. It didn't matter which one of us they were calling. It was always the same for us."

Trussi rubbed his head. 'This is not what I need or want. These three orphans, now runaways, could ruin everything! I have to think of what to do.' Trussi pondered their predicament.

Ferraro looked confused. "Trussi, you said that word earlier, dwarf. What does that mean?"

Trussi sighed. "It means little person. These other bigger people who we thought were giants are actually regular-sized. They are in every town and village outside of ours. Giants are real and far bigger than these people. But I think they live high up in the mountains. Anyway, these regular-sized people call us dwarves."

Doc interrupted by shouting from just ahead on the road. "Hey, I see the next town! It's not that far!"

Trussi was glad to hear that. "Good, we'll need to stock up on supplies. These three need sleeping blankets, travel shoes, food, and water."

Ferraro shook his head. "I don't know, Trussi, maybe we should think about...."

Trussi knew where he was going with this and didn't let him finish. "Think about what, going back to our town? And then what? You think our town will gladly accept three strangers with open arms?"

Trussi looked at the orphan who had spoken previously. "Do you three have any skills? Were you trained to make any trades, such as baking, pottery, or leather?"

He shook his head. Looking perplexed at Trussi's question, he continued, "The only thing we were ever trained to do was to perform as clowns in the carnival."

Trussi looked back at Ferraro. "If we go back, what do you think will happen to these three? Assuming that the carnival doesn't catch up to us, that is. I'll tell you what will happen. They'll become field workers. They'll work as hard as they can daily, barely making money to feed themselves. And, like everyone else who works in the field, one day they'll work themselves to death."

Ferraro looked upset. "Trussi, you don't know that will happen...."

Trussi continued, "Then tell me, what do you think will happen to three men without family, skills, money, or education? What do you think will come of them if we return to our town right now?"

Ferraro ran a hand through his hair, contemplating Trussi's words. He sucked in a deep breath, and his eyes turned away. "You are right, Trussi. Without family, stature, and skills, these three would only be able to find work in the fields." He looked over at the orphans, his face looking apologetic and sad.

Trussi had an idea just then, replacing his irritation. He placed a hand firmly on Ferraro's shoulder. "It's okay." Pausing momentarily, he turned to the orphans and crossed his arms. He didn't like the alternative but couldn't think of anything better.

"They can come with us if they want to. And if they want to go to our town or stay somewhere else, that is their choice." Trussi could feel the tension in the air. All three of the newcomers were staring at him wide-eyed.

Trussi sighed. "So what will it be? You can come with us if you want. We are seeking adventure and fortune out here in the big world. If you don't want to come with us, we can take you to a town somewhere, and you can take your chances. Either way, it's your choice."

The three turned to each other, whispering their discussion. The third one sneezed again, and Trussi wondered if this was a nervous habit or something he regularly did. They all nodded, apparently in agreement with each other.

"Okay, we'll come with you. But we each would like a share. However much treasure there, regardless of who finds it, we want to be a part of it." Like before, the shy orphan huddled behind the one that spoke, and the sneezy one nodded while sniffling.

Trussi didn't need any time to think. It was a fair request, and he nodded in agreement, as did Doc and Ferraro. Trussi wasn't happy about adding more people to the group but was relieved they were not heading back to Laus.

"Good. Let's head over to the town and get supplies. I want us all to leave before it's dark, as I don't want to stay longer than we have to. The longer we stay, the more attention we'll draw. Right now, we need to be as invisible as possible. Agreed?" Everyone agreed again.

With that, they headed towards the town. Doc was right. The town was just up ahead, and they quickly reached the entrance. Luckily, the gate was open, and they could enter without being noticed. Trussi hesitated before entering and took the group off to the side.

"What is it, Trussi?" Ferraro asked.

"We need to split up. We can gather supplies faster if one group gets sleep blankets and winter jackets while the other gets food and water supplies."

"I agree," Doc said. "I think one of the orphans, myself, and Remo should be one of the groups. We can gather the blankets and winter jackets if the rest of you want to get the food and water supplies."

Trussi nodded. "That should be fine. Make sure you get some winter shoes as well. The shoes those three have are pretty thin and severely worn."

Doc nodded his head but looked worried. "I agree they need new shoes, but I don't know if I have enough money for everything." Trussi had saved more than enough money for himself over the years. He reached into his pocket, pulled out some money, and handed that to Doc. Doc's surprise showed on his face, and he hurriedly slipped his funds into his right boot.

Ferraro sighed deeply. "Trussi, please don't tell me you keep all your money in your pocket!?"

Trussi shrugged his shoulders. "Most of it is in my pocket. That way, I can use it easily when I need it. The rest is in my travel bag."

Ferraro shook his head. "Trussi, we are going into an unfamiliar new town. There could be thieves and pickpockets here. It would be best if you were smarter about carrying your money. Should you get robbed, would you still have enough money to continue on this journey?"

Trussi's eyes furrowed in realization. 'How could I have been so careless!' At that very moment, he felt naïve and embarrassed.

Ferraro came over to him. "Look, Trussi, I keep my money in several different spots. Yes, I keep some of my money in my pocket, so should I be robbed, the thief will find this money easily and leave. The rest of my money is in several other places, such as a hidden pocket inside my travel pack and a hidden pocket in my jacket. Also, I keep money in my boots and a hidden pouch around my neck, nestled under my beard."

Trussi raised his eyebrows in surprise. Ferraro was well prepared. Deciding he wanted to be safer, Trussi pulled out some of the money he had in his pocket and placed it awkwardly in each of his boots. He decided he would have to find some material to make a few hidden pouches for himself.

"Okay, I'm all set. It should only take a couple of hours to purchase our supplies. Once done, we'll meet back here. I think it is best to leave the same way we came in to give an impression we headed back the way we came. I know it'll add to today's journey, walking around the town to continue traveling north. But it will be worth it if it throws the caravan off our track." The others passively agreed and started getting ready to head into town.

"Wait!" Trussi called out. "Before we go in, we need to discuss just one more thing. These three don't have names." Trussi gestured towards the three orphans.

No one responded, so he started the process. He pointed to the shy orphan, "We can call you Loris." He then gestured to the one constantly sneezing, "You can be called Dante." Trussi then pointed to the third orphan, but he responded by calling out his name before Trussi could say anything.

"Marco! I want to be called Marco." Trussi wouldn't have chosen that name, but if he wanted to be called Marco, then so be it.

"Okay, fine, Marco, it is." Trussi then looked at Doc. "Is everyone ready to go into town?" Doc and everyone else nodded and stood up to walk into the town.

Trussi said, "Glad that is all settled. Doc, you stay here with Remo and Marco. The rest of us will go in first, and then you can enter in a few minutes. We'll meet back here when everyone is finished shopping." Trussi stood up and headed into the town with Ferraro, Dante, and Loris. They headed towards the town center, where the open markets were sure to be.

They walked for a bit, getting weird looks from the townspeople. It dawned on Trussi that these people had probably never seen a dwarf. They kept as low a profile as possible, wanting to avoid drawing too much attention. They quickly made it to the center of the town, where a large market with many peddlers was bustling with activity. Ferraro looked concerned. "How will we find what we need in all this chaos?"

Trussi slapped him on the back with a smile. "We just follow the scent of food!" He smelled the air, taking a slow deep breath through his nose. "Okay, this way!" They followed the delicious scent, which led to several food peddlers.

Trussi first went to a food vendor selling different kinds of meats. The meat roasting on the fire smelled so good he couldn't resist passing it up. He purchased enough to share among the group for that evening's meal. He also bought more jerky and hard tack for three newcomers.

From there, they went to another vendor selling leather items, and Trussi bought three travel packs, some material to make himself secret money pockets, and a small sack just like Ferraro's. He then purchased three more travel flasks from another vendor.

Trussi noticed a well in the middle of the market where people drew water. He had Loris and Dante fill the three flasks and his own while he went to the vendor selling fresh fruits and vegetables. Trussi normally bartered, but since he wanted to avoid drawing attention to himself, he paid the total asking price for the items he selected.

Finally, Trussi knew they would need additional axes, shovels, and pickaxes, so he looked for the local blacksmith. It took a while for them to find the shop. When they did find it, they were shocked at the sizes of the tools. Everything was larger-scale than what Trussi and Ferraro were used to since nothing in this shop was intended for dwarves. He sighed, looking through the assortment of items. They eventually picked out the smallest ones he and Ferraro could find. Ferraro also found some smaller knives and added that to the purchase.

They were about to return to the entrance when they passed a merchant selling clothing. Trussi looked at Loris and Dante. Their clothes were tattered and filthy. Besides needing warmer clothes for the winter, they also needed new shoes for traveling. Trussi had the merchant look over Loris and Dante, getting their sizes. They fit into children's clothing, of course, but it was far better than what they had on before. He bought a third set to give to Marco before they left.

Once finished, they reached the town's entrance without any trouble and waited on the side of the road for the other group to return. They made small talk as they waited. And after an hour, with no sign of the others, Trussi and Ferraro became concerned.

"Do you think we should go looking for them?" Trussi said as he started to pace nervously.

Ferraro shook his head. "No, let's give them a few more minutes. We'll look for them if they aren't back by then."

Some more time went by, and Trussi anxiously stood up. "Okay, I'm done waiting. Let's look for them. Hopefully, they haven't gotten into trouble."

Just as they started to enter the town, Dante saw Doc and the rest of the other group. "Look, there they are!"

Trussi and Ferraro both sighed with relief.

Doc apologized as the two groups joined together. "I'm sorry we are late. The marketplace was so big that we had difficulty finding everything we needed."

Everyone set out the new things they had purchased: shoes, coats, sleeping sacks, and travel gear. Trussi gave the clothes and flasks he bought to Marco. All three orphans filled their travel bags with their new belongings. Once everything was organized and packed, the group continued walking around the town's border towards the north.

As they made their way, Trussi kept everyone just beyond the border under the shade of the trees, so they remained unperceived. There was no trail, so walking was more complex and slower than expected. After several hours, they finally reached the northern entrance to the town. There was a wide cobblestone road leading north, and now they could walk on the road without any concern about footprints. As they continued north, the town slowly shrank into the distance behind them.

Once the sky started to darken, they walked away from the road to make camp. Trussi wanted to walk far enough so anyone still traveling on the road could not see their campfire. Once he was sure they were a safe distance away, they all set up camp for the night and got a small fire going.

Before going to sleep, Trussi handed out the cooked meat he had purchased earlier that day. It tasted as delicious as it smelled, and everyone enjoyed it heartily. That night, with their bellies full, they relaxed and enjoyed the warmth of the fire. The seven dwarves all slept very well that night.

CH. 13 TREASURED GIFTS

Birds were singing as the sun rose above the hillside. The fire had burned itself out. But, despite this, everyone seemed to have gotten plenty of rest. Trussi got ready, and everyone quickly got underway. They returned to the cobblestone road and headed north again. The weather was slightly chilly compared to the day before, with murky clouds keeping the sky colored gray. The entire morning the sky continued to darken with thick clouds. As midday approached, the sky let loose, and the rain fell heavily and continuously.

As the end of the day approached, Ferraro spotted a town not far ahead. They all agreed it would be good to stay at an inn for the night as they were all thoroughly soaked. As they approached, Trussi realized that he was nearly out of money. After giving Doc some funds and purchasing all the additional supplies, he wasn't sure he had enough to pay for an inn, especially now that there were seven of them.

This situation got him thinking about his pickaxe. Strega had told him it would bring him a fortune no matter where he used this or what it struck. If it could bring him wealth, he would have to use it secretly, away from the others. Just as they got to the town, they discovered the front entrance was gated, and the large wooden doors were closed. Ferraro knocked, and a small window opened with a skinny dirty man peering out.

"Who goes there? State your business!" The dirty man sounded gruff and looked irritated.

Ferraro shouted back. "We are travelers and seek shelter for the night. Our business is only to sleep at an inn, and then we'll leave first thing in the morning!"

The dirty man in the window huffed and eyed them suspiciously. After a moment, they heard the gate unlatch, and the large wooden gates opened slowly.

"You may stay for the night, but you'd better be able to pay for the inn, or you'll be strung up by your tiny little feet!" He smiled wickedly at them, chuckling to himself.

They walked through the gate, knowing that any inn would be towards the center of town, close to the markets. They could see an open inn that looked like it had room for them as they approached.

Before entering, Trussi paused. "I uh... I have to relieve myself before I go in."

Doc was tired and moaned at Trussi then. "Oh, come on! Just hold it and go once we get a room!" But Doc's agitation only fueled Trussi's irritation.

"I cannot wait! This will only take a moment!" He immediately started walking to the back of the inn towards the dark alley. He didn't wait for anyone else to distract him from his secret intent.

He looked around, making sure that he was indeed alone. Taking his pickaxe, he held it with both hands. He wasn't sure what he should try to strike, and he looked around. Finding a worn wooden box, he figured that would be easy enough to try. Trussi took a deep breath, letting it out slowly. He closed his eyes as he lifted the pickaxe. It tingled in his hands as if it knew what he would do. Swinging the pickaxe lightly, he hit the box with gentle force. Trussi immediately opened his eyes and stared in shock.

There, before him, on the box where the pickaxe had struck, was a brassy yellow-gold nugget. It was rough looking, misshapen, and nearly the size of his palm. He picked it up, finding it was cool to the touch. It was also heavier than it looked, and Trussi turned it over, looking at it from side to side.

"Hey, Trussi!! Are you done yet?" Doc shouted towards him. Trussi shoved the gold into his pocket and quickly placed his pickaxe back in his travel pack.

"Yes, I'm done!" Trussi called back as he walked back towards them. The group had already entered the inn, and Trussi was the last to join them. Ferraro finished talking with Doc and walked over to him with a worried look.

"Trussi, how much money do you have left? Doc and I have put the remaining money together, and it's not enough."

Trussi smiled knowingly and patted him on the shoulder. "Relax, I got this." He walked up to the innkeeper. "I'm sorry, I missed the price of the room. How much was it?"

The innkeeper looked irritated but stated the price again. Trussi nodded his head as if contemplating what was said. After a moment, he smiled and reached into his pocket. "Okay, that won't be a problem. However, my companions and I will require two of your rooms instead of one. And we'll need hot baths and hot soup to fill our bellies."

The innkeeper furrowed his eyes. "And exactly how do you expect to pay for everything?" His tone was calm but hinted at irritation.

Trussi presented the gold nugget from his pocket and couldn't help but have a smug look on his face. "I trust that this will be an adequate payment?"

The innkeeper looked shocked and stood there momentarily, not saying anything. Finally, he collected his wits, and he was able to speak. "Yes.... YES! That is more than adequate. Thank you, Sir." He snatched the nugget from Trussi's hand and turned to test the gold by biting it. He then called out for one of his workers.

"Show these fine gentlemen to their rooms!" He turned back to Trussi, smiling. "Would you gentlemen care to eat now or bathe first?"

Trussi shivered. He was soaked and cold to the bone, and so were the rest of the dwarves. "We would like our hot baths first, please."

The innkeeper smiled politely. "Certainly, Sir. My man will show you to your rooms. When you are ready, he will show you to the bathhouse, where your hot baths will be ready and waiting for you." Trussi nodded toward the innkeeper, and he nodded back.

They followed the attendant up some stairs and to their two rooms. The beds were for full-sized adults, but to the dwarves, the beds were enormous! They immediately started peeling off their wet coats and shoes, hanging them to dry.

Ferraro grabbed Trussi, pulling him off to the side in a rigid and jerking motion. "Okay, Trussi, where did you get that gold?" His voice was low and quiet, but he looked and sounded angry.

Trussi didn't want to lie to Ferraro but was unsure what to tell him. He kept his voice low so the others couldn't hear. "I don't know if you'll believe me."

Ferraro scowled. "Don't you dare lie to me!"

Trussi realized that Ferraro thought he had stolen the gold. He shook his head. "It's not what you think. I did not steal anything."

Ferraro still appeared upset. "Then where did it come from!" His anger got the best of him, and the others looked at them with concern.

Before Trussi could answer, they were interrupted by an attendant holding some dry towels. "Here are your towels, gentlemen. Your hot baths are now ready."

Ferraro shook his head. "This discussion is not over. We all need baths, but after we have bathed, you will explain yourself."

"After we bathe and eat, I'll explain everything." Trussi corrected.

Ferraro didn't say anything. Instead, he turned around, grabbed a towel from the attendant, and removed his remaining wet clothes. They followed the attendant down the stairs to the bathhouse behind the inn. Once they entered the bathhouse, heat, and steam surrounded them. The room was reasonably large, with wooden walls and wooden floors. The center had four large bathtubs, each steaming with hot water.

Trussi put his hand in one of them. The water was hot, but it felt amazing! He didn't hesitate. He let his towel fall to the floor, and he jumped in. The others paired up and entered the bathtubs. They were not made for dwarves, as the baths were big enough for two or three dwarves. Trussi had his bath all to himself and sank into the water, enveloping himself in the warmth.

Trussi could hear the satisfying groans and moans of the others as they were also warming up and relaxing in the wondrous hot water. He smiled to himself, feeling very relaxed. After a while, an attendant came in with steaming buckets of fresh hot water and added them to the baths to help keep them hot. Trussi decided he could easily sleep in the tub if there weren't a chance of drowning. He closed his eyes, stretching out his tired body as the soreness dissipated slowly. 'I could assuredly get used to this.' He happily thought.

Over the next several hours, several attendants brought hot water to freshen the baths. Finally, an attendant announced that their hot meal was ready. Trussi noticed his hands and feet were wrinkled, and he was finally ready to leave the bath.

The group headed slowly back to their rooms to dress. Once they were ready, the attendant led everyone to the dining area, where seven bowls of steaming hot soup were waiting at a long table. There were also small fresh loaves of bread on the table with butter and a knife beside each loaf.

They each took a chair, which was awkward as they were made for much larger people. No one hesitated and immediately started eating. After several spoonfuls, Trussi tossed his spoon to the side. He picked up his bowl and started gulping down the soup. Everyone else started doing the same, and the soup disappeared within moments. Using a piece of the bread to clean his bowl, Trussi had no drop of soup remaining. The bread was fresh and soft and tasted fantastic with the soup tailings. It didn't take long to finish the remaining bread. Soon, everyone started yawning, and Trussi saw they were ready for sleep.

They thanked the attendants and headed back upstairs to their rooms. As everyone was heading to one of the beds, Trussi was pulled away to the side by Ferraro. Trussi groaned. He was just as tired as the rest and wanted to join them in sleep.

"Can't this wait till morning?" he complained.

Ferraro kept his voice low and quiet. "No, this can't."

Trussi grumbled, "Fine. But we need to wait for everyone to fall asleep first."

Ferraro nodded his head in agreement. Luckily it didn't take long before they heard the snores of their companions sleeping.

Ferraro glared at Trussi. "Alright, no more delays. You need to tell me where you got that gold."

Trussi swallowed hard. He kept his voice low and quiet in case the innkeeper or one of the attendants snooped and tried to listen in. "Do you remember when I told you about Strega?"

Ferraro looked surprised but nodded his head. "Well, there was one thing I didn't tell you."

Trussi closed his eyes and sighed. "Shortly after we started talking, she asked for my pickaxe. I can't explain why, but I handed it to her. She said some words I didn't understand and then returned the pickaxe to me. She told me that she had just enchanted it, so I would find treasure no matter what it struck. She also said it would only work for me, so if anyone else were to use it, the magic would not work."

Ferraro was upset in many ways. "And you didn't think to tell me this until now?!"

Trussi lowered his head and spoke even more softly. "I wasn't sure it would work. This evening was the first time I had tried using it. I know how most people feel about witchcraft. And, to be honest, I was worried that you would have made me discard it if I had told you. I can't explain it, but I have felt connected with my pickaxe since Strega placed her enchantment.

"Not only that, but I would be to blame if we cannot find treasure or riches by the time this adventure is finished. I don't want to let everyone down."

Ferraro closed his eyes while clenching his fists. He took a deep breath, letting it out slowly as he considered everything. "Trussi, I don't ever want you to keep important information like this from me again." Ferraro sighed, though his eyes still showed intense anger.

"You are right. I would have made you abandon it at that time. Witch magic is something you want to avoid getting involved in. But you have used it now. I wouldn't discard it. Also, it may cause others in the group to wonder about you leaving it behind.

"Also, we should keep this information to ourselves. I don't want the others to worry about witch magic or think our trek is cursed."

Trussi was surprised but glad to have Ferraro agree not to involve the others in this knowledge.

"One more thing." Ferraro looked around, making sure no prying eyes were around. "I may not be the only one who thought you a thief. The innkeeper looked surprised to see that gold, and I doubt he has ever seen that much of it at one time. If he suspects we have stolen it from somewhere, he could alert a sheriff in the morning, who could retain us for questioning. If you can't tell him how some measly little peasants like us got gold like that, we could be locked up or worse!"

"Oh..." Trussi felt his stomach drop.

Ferraro nodded. "I think it is best to leave early in the morning before much of the town has woken up. We need to leave the way we came in, and once the town is out of sight, we can head north again."

Trussi nodded. "Okay. I like that plan."

Ferraro went to his travel bag, pulling out a long rolled paper. He brought it over to Trussi and unrolled it. It was a map of the kingdom!

"Where did you get this?!"

Trussi was aghast. He had planned on purchasing a map, but by freeing the orphans and then adding them to their group, he had long since forgotten.

"I bought this at the last town we visited when you bought clothes for the other three." He pointed to a town on the map. "Look, we are here. We can easily go around this way." He directed his finger around the city, which appeared bigger on the map than the last town. "We can continue going north this way. As we continue on this route, there will be several more towns, but right here..." He pointed to a high spot on the map, "...the main road intersects one last time. If we continue north, we'll go directly to the queen's castle. We already know we don't want to go there, so we should decide now whether to go east or west."

Trussi eyed the map, looking at the adjacent towns. Once the road split where Ferraro had pointed, there was only one town in both directions and nothing but woods surrounding the mountain range to the edge of the map.

Trussi then went to his travel bag and pulled out his book. He flipped through the pages until he found the description of where the characters had started mining. "Look! See right here..." Trussi pointed to the map east of the queen's castle. "...look at the mountain ranges formation. The shape and positioning are exactly like it is in my book! This is where we'll travel to."

Ferraro rolled his eyes. "Trussi, you can't plan everything based on that dumb book of yours."

Instantly irritated, Trussi retorted, "This is not some 'dumb book.' This was my grandmother's book! And I never asked you or anyone else to join me on this journey of mine! This is where I am going. I can't explain, but I must go to this spot." Trussi pointed to the same spot on the map again. "If you think this is so dumb, you are welcome to leave. I can do this on my own."

Ferraro shook his head. "That's not what I meant, Trussi. I meant that this is not just your adventure. This is our adventure. That book isn't real. But this is real, you and me and them." He pointed to the others sleeping in the beds.

Trussi closed his eyes, swallowing down his anger. "I don't expect you to understand. But I feel like this is my destiny. This is where I am meant to go, where I am meant to be." Trussi shook his head and sighed. "I understand your hesitation. If you want to part ways, I will not blame or hold any ill will against you."

Ferraro's eyes furrowed as he frowned and crossed his arms. "You are not getting rid of me that easily. If you believe, without a doubt, that this is where we need to go, then I'm with you all the way."

Trussi smiled and nodded his head. "I am sure without a doubt that this is where I need to go."

Ferraro nodded back at him and uncrossed his arms. Despite planning to be on this adventure alone, Trussi was glad Ferraro was with him. Reviewing the journey, he accepted he was glad they were all there with him.

Ferraro looked tired and let out an exhausted yawn. Trussi was no longer tired and felt too worked up to sleep.

"Why don't you go to sleep first? I will keep watch and alert everyone if I sense any trouble. Once half the night is finished, I'll wake you up to take over my watch."

Ferraro nodded and yawned again. "I like that plan."

He patted Trussi on the shoulder and climbed into bed. It wasn't long until he fell asleep and started snoring loudly. Trussi looked out the window, keeping watch for anything suspicious. Hours passed, and nothing seemed to be happening. He finally felt tired and went to wake up Ferraro. He pushed on his shoulders, but that only made his snoring louder.

"Come on, Ferraro. Get up. It's your turn to keep watch."

His snoring finally stopped, and he coughed as he sat up. "Wh-what's going on?..."

"Nothing is going on. It's been quiet the whole time, with no one coming or going. Come on, get up. It's your turn to keep watch. I need to get some sleep!"

Ferraro nodded his head and pushed the covers off of himself. Trussi crawled into the same bed, pulling the warm covers over his tired body. He immediately drifted off into a deep, dreamless sleep.

The clanking of workers washing dishes woke Trussi up from

his deep slumber. Someone was washing dishes rather loudly downstairs. He could see a little bit of daylight coming through the window, and the snores of everyone around him surrounded him. Trussi closed his eyes, still tired.

'Weren't we going to get up early to leave?' he suddenly thought. Trussi jolted up, startling himself awake. 'We overslept!!' He looked over to Ferraro, who had fallen asleep at the window.

"Ferraro, wake up! Wake up, damn you!" Trussi grabbed Ferraro's shoulder, shaking him gently awake. Ferraro woke up with a start, looking around.

Realization sank in, and his face paled with fear. "Oh, no! I fell asleep while keeping watch."

Trussi was in too much of a hurry to chastise him. "That doesn't matter now. We must pack and get out of here as fast as possible!"

They both quickly and quietly roused the others. Luckily, everyone got packed and ready with little questioning or complaints. Once prepared, everyone started heading down the stairs. Unfortunately, the stairs were made of wood and very creaky as they walked.

Even though they were in a rush to leave, Trussi walked carefully down the steps taking time to be as quiet as possible. Luckily the entrance was pretty close, and they reached the front door.

Trussi was relieved. They had all left, apparently unnoticed. They navigated the town quickly, heading back the same way they had come. It was still early, and few people were up, so the streets were mostly empty.

They reached the front gate again, finding it closed and locked. Trussi cursed under his breath. He had forgotten about the gatekeeper. As they approached, he saw the same man from last night step out. "Good morning! Where are you going so early in the morning?"

Ferraro stepped forward. "We told you last night that we are travelers and would leave in the morning. It is now morning, and we must continue on our journey."

The man nodded and yawned. He appeared unconcerned as he unlatched the gate. He opened it barely enough for each of them to fit through, and it was closed loudly once they were all outside the gate.

'Good.' Trussi thought. 'Since they locked the gate behind us, no one may be interested in following us.' The group started heading south, and after a while, Doc had some questions.

"I hate to point out the obvious, but we are traveling back the same way we came."

"That is true, Doc," Ferraro said as they walked.

Doc scoffed. "Okay, so why are we walking back in the same direction we came from? And why did we have to leave in such a hurry?"

Ferraro answered, "We left hurriedly because we didn't want to draw attention. The last thing we must do is draw attention to ourselves wherever we go. Also, we are traveling in the same direction we came from for the same reasons we did before. Should the carnival come this way and ask about any dwarves who have traveled in this direction, anyone who did see us will tell them we traveled south."

Trussi liked the explanation Ferraro had given. It wasn't the entire truth, but it was still an honest explanation of their situation. Once the town was out of sight, they turned north to head around the city, keeping out of view of the town. Ferraro led the way, using his map to help guide the group. It took most of the day to go around the town until they finally reached the road again. Continuing north, they walked until it got dark. Like before, they moved well away from the road to make their camp.

Trussi built a small fire, and everyone circled it for warmth. The group's morale was high, and everyone spoke about the glorious warm baths they had back in the town and what they wanted to do during and after this adventure they were on. Once again, seven dwarves slept peacefully by a fire in the woods.

CH. 14 BEWARE THE QUEEN

The group awoke come morning and continued traveling north, retaking the cobblestone road. Trussi was relieved that today had better weather as the sun came out and the sky was crystal clear. As the day progressed north, the road started twisting and turning, getting more and more curved as they walked. Ferraro stopped at midday to recheck his map and their location.

Everyone was glad for the rest, and as Ferraro checked his map, Trussi pulled out the last of the produce he had purchased several days ago, and everyone enjoyed the snack. Once Ferraro finally decided they were on track, they continued traveling north again. As they were walking, the group occasionally passed other travelers headed south. They got a couple of weird glances from the other travelers but other than that, no one seemed to care about their group, and they mostly ignored them.

The end of the day came quickly, and they made camp like normal. The next few days went about the same, and they made their way north without hiccups. It took four more days before they reached the next town, and they only stopped briefly to restock on water and essential food items.

While restocking their supplies, Trussi heard several townsfolk passing on strange rumors about the queen regarding her beauty and cruelty. It made Trussi uneasy when he listened to the villagers speaking about the queen, which reminded him of the warning he had gotten from Strega. His resolve strengthened to steer clear of her, and once restocked, they left quickly, continuing on their journey north.

The next day, the sky had turned gray again, and the smell of coming rain loomed in the air. It didn't rain the entire day, but it started pouring just as they set up camp for the night. No town was in sight, and, according to the map, the next town was still several days' walk ahead.

So they made the best of it, trying to keep everything they had and themselves under dense tree coverage. They huddled together to stay warm, as starting a campfire was impossible with everything soaked. That night, sleep was restless, and each was weary come morning. The rain had stopped, but the muddy ground made the trek more difficult for now.

It didn't rain again for the next three days, but it remained overcast and cold. They were exhausted, wet, and freezing when they reached the next town. They entered the city, restocking their supplies at the large central market. Trussi could see numerous inns, and they each looked very inviting.

Even though it wasn't dark, the group started discussing their desire to stay at one of the local inns. Everyone wanted to clean themselves up and finally get warm and dry again. Ferraro pulled Trussi aside as the others were talking.

"The prices at this market are considerably higher than in previous towns. I am concerned that staying at one of the inns will be more expensive too. If it is, I don't think we will have enough money to stay." He paused briefly, looking around to ensure no one was listening in. "So, I think you need to use your pickaxe, Trussi."

Trussi raised his eyebrows. "I already did. I wanted to ensure I was ready before we reached the town." Trussi pulled out several tiny pieces of gold, showing them to Ferraro.

Ferraro examined them, saying, "They are smaller than the last piece of gold, which is good. I think it's best to avoid attracting attention, so I will take these to the local blacksmith's shop and trade them for coins. I think this will be more discreet, and we passed by a blacksmith's shop not long ago. It's not far behind us. Tell the others I'll be right back." Trussi agreed, and Ferraro swiftly left.

"Where is Ferraro?" Doc asked when he noticed Ferraro leaving.

"He'll be back soon. He went to the blacksmith's shop first." Trussi said casually.

Sill concerned, Doc questioned. "Why did he go there? I thought we were getting a room at one of the inns?" Doc asked while looking concerned.

Trussi paused as he didn't want to lie, but he couldn't tell them the entire truth either. "We are getting a room. He just needed.... to trade something with the blacksmith first. This way, we will have enough money to pay for the inn."

Doc's eyes furrowed. "I didn't know that we were low on money. I hope he isn't trading something important."

Trussi shook his head. "No, he's not trading something important."

Everyone waited patiently, and Ferraro returned quickly. Trussi told him what he had informed the others, just in case anyone asked what he had traded. They entered a little inn and walked up to the front desk. Ferraro was in the front of the group as they approached the front desk.

The man behind the front desk was clean, well-dressed, and plump. His dark hair was combed, showing streaks of gray. He smiled at them as they approached. It was the type of smile you make when putting up with someone you wish would disappear.

"Good afternoon, gentlemen. How may I help you?" His words

were polite, but his tone was condescending.

Ferraro smiled politely back. "We would like two rooms, please. And, if it's not too much trouble, could you tell me the price of hot baths and a meal for the seven of us? As you can see, we have been traveling and need cleaning up."

The man at the front desk gave them a price for everything, and Ferraro had been right. The prices here were considerably steeper than they had been previously.

Ferraro nodded at the man. "That will be fine. We'll take it."

The man looked surprised as if he had expected them to argue over the price or just up and leave. "Very good, sirs. However, my cook is sick for the day. You'll have to go to the market to find a meal. Also, I expect full payment before you tend to your rooms." He smiled again, showing crooked teeth within his pudgy features.

"Certainly." Ferraro reached into his pocket and drew enough money to pay the tab. The man behind the desk smiled even more prominent.

"My staff will show you to your rooms. We need to start warming the water for your baths. They won't be ready for a while yet."

Ferraro waved his hand in a dismissive gesture. "That's fine. Just have one of your staff inform us when the baths are ready."

From there, a staff member showed them to their rooms. This inn was of higher quality than the last one they had stayed. There were more ornate fixtures, the wooden floors were not creaky, and the beds smelled fresh and clean.

Ferraro turned to Trussi. "I have a bit of money left over. I'm too tired to go, but can you go to the market and pick up some fresh food for dinner? We all need a break from eating jerky and travel food."

Trussi was just as tired but agreed they needed better food

tonight. "Not a problem."

"Take Doc with you." Ferraro quickly suggested as he handed Trussi the remaining money. "It's best not to go alone."

Doc groaned. "Ugh. I just sat down. My legs are aching so badly. Why not take Marco or Dante?" Both Marco and Dante groaned at that suggestion. Everyone was equally exhausted.

Trussi sighed. "It's fine. I can manage the market by myself." Trussi got a disapproving look from Ferraro.

"Look, I even made this secret money pouch several days ago. It's just like yours." Trussi pulled out the small sack he had nestled under his chin and beard and put the money inside. He had made it a while back when he was having difficulty sleeping.

Ferraro shook his head. "I don't like the idea of anyone going out alone."

Trussi snorted. "You went to the blacksmith's shop alone."

Ferraro sighed, "That was very nearby, and I was only gone for a few minutes. This is different."

It was then that Trussi noticed Remo holding his hand up. He started smiling once Trussi saw him. "You want to come with me?" If this ended the argument, Trussi would take him. Remo nodded emphatically.

"Fine!! It's settled. Let's go!!" Trussi got up and left before anyone could argue. He wanted to get to the market and return quickly, so he wouldn't miss his chance to take a hot bath.

Remo followed quickly behind. They entered the market, and Trussi sniffed the air, seeking the smell of fresh food. He followed a delicious scent to a stand roasting pork over a fire. He asked about the price, and though it was higher than expected, Trussi couldn't help but purchase the delicious-smelling food. Once he had paid for the meat, Trussi's stomach grumbled up at him with intense hunger. He looked over at Remo, who looked just as hungry as he felt.

"It wouldn't hurt to eat some while it's fresh... What do you think? Should we have some right now or wait to eat with the others?" Remo gave him a broad smile and held out his hands.

They shared some of the freshly cooked meat, enjoying every bite. It was incredibly tender and very, very tasty. Trussi then saw the baker's stand. He couldn't help but buy several loaves of fresh bread and some butter to go with it. Before they did anything else, Trussi tore off several pieces of the bread, sharing it with Remo.

"Well, that's it. That was the last of my money. Let's return to the others and enjoy the hot baths with them." Remo nodded, and they started back towards the inn.

They didn't get very far when they heard Trumpets blasting. Someone then shouted, "The queen!! The queen!!! Queen Regina approaches!!!!"

A horse-drawn carriage burst into the middle of the market all at once. People were scrambling to get out of the way. Trussi could hear people screaming as they were pushed aside in the frantic frenzy. Trussi grabbed Remo by the arm, pulling him behind a large stand to avoid getting trampled. After a moment, the screams and running people stopped, and all went silent. Trussi peaked around the corner to look at the carriage, which had stopped in the center of the marketplace.

A fancifully-dressed man standing at the front of the carriage stepped off and shouted: "Her royal majesty, Queen Regina!!"

Trussi's stomach dropped, and he felt the hairs on the back of his neck stand on end. The carriage door opened, and a woman slowly stepped out. If he had said she was beautiful, he would have been lying. She was more than beautiful. She was ravishing! He wasn't sure how that was possible, but there she was!

She wore several jeweled necklaces, multiple golden rings, and a crown. She was adorned with lovely golden-brown wavy hair that cascaded down her back. Her clothes were silky smooth with deeply colored purples, teal blues, and pale pink accents. Her skin was flawless, with lips that were deep pink and pouty. Lastly, her eyes were a vibrant green color. They were so green that Trussi thought they almost seemed to glow....

As she stepped out of the carriage, she adjusted her delicate dress and the crown atop her head, ensuring everything was perfect. She started walking forward slowly. As she took her first steps, Trussi heard the gasps of several men around him exclaiming in surprise at how beautiful she was.

'No wonder she is renowned for her beauty.' he thought. 'She is more beautiful than anyone I've ever seen!' Remembering Strega's warning, he tried to turn his eyes away to leave. But, at that very moment, the queen's eyes suddenly turned and looked directly at him. Her expression didn't change, but she shifted her feet and slowly walked straight toward him.

The hairs on his neck intensified the tingling sensation which ran down his back and to his toes. 'Oh crap! I need to get out of here!' he thought in panic. Trussi still couldn't take his gaze off her. She only took about five or six steps toward him when a man wearing royal guard armor approached her.

He bowed before speaking, saying quietly, "My queen, we have found the girl. She is this way." He pointed away from Trussi to another part of the town. Her gaze shifted from Trussi to the guard, and when her eyes turned, Trussi found he could move again. He turned away, retracting himself and gasping for air. He had not even realized he had been holding his breath.

He could hear the guard walking away and hoped the queen was going with him. Trussi dared not look back as he had no desire to look into those intense green eyes again. Remo was still next to him and looked scared. Trussi patted his hand, trying to comfort him.

"It's going to be okay. But we got to get back to the others."

He looked around, trying to see which direction the inn was. After a moment, he noticed a back alley and headed through there. It would take longer to go around the marketplace to return to the inn, but Trussi wanted to avoid the queen and her guards. They both started as quickly as they could.

Trussi was initially worried Remo would fall behind but was glad Remo could keep up just fine as they jetted between alleyways and streets. As they were dashing around, they also were trying to be as low-key and invisible as possible. Both were walking fast and dodging everyone, trying to stay unnoticed. Trussi got a little lost while walking quickly and soon realized he was unfamiliar with his surroundings.

Trussi suddenly stopped dead in his tracks. Directly in front of him, at the end of the alley, was the queen and two of her guards! He started to back up quietly and quickly. Trussi turned around the corner out of sight and released a deep breath.

'Crap! How do I get out of here? Perhaps we should go back the way we came?' As he looked around, he heard the sobbing of a young girl. Trussi didn't want to look but couldn't help but peek around the corner toward the sound. He saw a young girl standing between the queen and her two guards. She was very young, perhaps thirteen or fourteen years old, and sobbed into her hands.

"Please....please..." She cried, "...I just want to go home." She looked up from her hands, pleading with the queen. Despite the dirty rags the girl wore and the tears pouring from her blue eyes, Trussi could tell she was quite pretty. She was more than pretty. She was absolutely lovely. Her golden hair hung in ringlets, her lips were a perfect heart shape, and her skin was a pale perfect porcelain color. Next to her, the queen didn't look near as ravishing as she had before.

The queen folded her arms, raising her head to look down at the girl. "My dear child, I cannot forgive this."

More tears fell from the girl as she pleaded, "But ... I haven't done anything!"

The queen bent close to the girl, her lips curling into a sneer. "There can only be one fairest in the land!" the queen hissed.

The queen looked as if she wanted to slap the girl. Instead, she looked up at the guard behind the girl and nodded. The guard slightly nodded back to the queen and shifted his position. His hand quickly wrapped around the girl's mouth as he raised his other hand, holding a knife. He drove it deep into her back, and Trussi heard a muffled scream. He immediately turned away in horror.

'She's crazy, absolutely crazy!!' He felt fear in the pit of his stomach, and, feeling the need to flee, he grabbed Remo's hand and bolted into the adjacent alleyway. Trussi was running now as his heart was beating intensely in his chest. 'I must tell the others and get us far away from here!

They finally made it back to the inn, and as Trussi entered, he saw the others walking down the stairs to the baths. Trussi ran up to Ferraro.

"Oh good!" Ferraro said with a smile. "You made it back in time! Our hot baths are ready!"

Trussi shook his head. "We need to talk right now!"

"Can we talk in the bathhouse?" Ferraro asked.

"No, we have to talk NOW!" Trussi did not want to fret the others and kept his voice low. "This is beyond important!"

Ferraro sighed, clearly frustrated. He looked over and saw the look on Remo's face. "Fine." He turned to the rest of the group. "You guys go on ahead. We'll join you in a moment." The three then headed to their room while the other four appeared concerned as they headed to the bathhouse.

Trussi didn't want to split up the group, but he hadn't discussed anything with them about his meeting with Strega or the warnings he had gotten about the queen. It would be best to talk with Ferraro first. Once they entered the room, Ferraro shut the door.

"Okay, what's going on, Trussi? Did you guys get into some trouble at the market?"

"No, it's nothing like that!" Trussi tried to gather his shaken wits. "I am going to tell you everything that just happened. But I need you to be quiet and listen, alright?"

Ferraro nodded, and Trussi proceeded to tell him everything that had happened. He was still shaken up but could still convey everything from the queen's coach crashing into the marketplace to what he saw happen in the alleyway. Ferraro listened intently, and when Trussi finished, Ferraro appeared worried.

"Are you sure she killed the girl?"

Trussi rolled his eyes. "She had her guard kill the girl. I saw him plunge the knife into her back, and I heard her scream!! I didn't stay around to check her pulse if that is what you're asking!" Trussi couldn't help but be upset. Everything about what happened was wrong. So very wrong.

Ferraro looked concerned and started to pace. "When she had the girl killed, did she see you in the alleyway?"

Trussi shook his head. "I don't think so, but I'm not sure. Maybe. We got out of there as fast as we could."

Remo nodded at this comment. Ferraro closed his eyes and rubbed his temples. "I need to think for a moment." He sighed, furrowing his eyes. After what felt like an exaggerated pause, he finally spoke again. "So it seems like the queen is here, not because of you but because of the girl. Didn't you say in your conversation with Strega that the queen will kill anyone who rivals her beauty?"

Trussi nodded, recalling the conversation with Strega. "Yes, she did say that."

"Then, perhaps she will leave the town now that she did what she came to do. I should check to see if the queen is still in town or if she has left. If she is still here, we will leave immediately. However, if she has already left, I would prefer to stay as our rooms are paid for, and everyone needs a good night's rest."

Trussi didn't like this plan at all. "Why wait? We should leave now!" he said impatiently.

Ferraro put his hand up in the air, his palm facing Trussi. "I understand what you have witnessed is traumatic, but don't let your fear cause you to panic and make a rash decision. What will it look like if the seven of us sneak off, having already paid for our expensive rooms? It will look like we are running from trouble, that's what! Trust me. Be patient. Let me check to see if the queen has left the city or has stayed. If she is still here, I promise you we will leave."

Trussi still didn't like it but trusted Ferraro with his life and nodded in agreement.

Ferraro smiled then. "While I am out in the town checking on the queen, why don't you two go take your hot baths? No need to waste hot water. I'll be back as quickly as I can." Ferraro headed out without hesitation.

Trussi took Remo downstairs to the bathing room. Like the other inn, the bathing room had wooden floors, wooden walls, and a wooden ceiling. However, there were five baths instead of four. The moment they entered, Trussi and Remo were engulfed by hot steam.

Trussi took a towel folded on a small table by the door and went to one of the empty baths. He removed his clothes quickly and climbed into the steaming water. It was hot and felt amazing, but his nerves and stress prevented him from relaxing. Remo hopped into the tub with him. He smiled as he seemed to relax better than Trussi did. Trussi had hoped Remo would have gotten into one of the other tubs, but it was too late to make that suggestion. Luckily, the tubs were for normal-sized people, not dwarves, and they easily fit within it, having room to spare.

Remo was relaxed, despite everything they had just gone through. Trussi closed his eyes and let out a big sigh. He knew he needed patience, but it was always difficult for him. He sat in the tub, trying to calm his nerves. After a short while, Ferraro returned. Trussi was surprised to see him so quickly and stood up to get out of the tub. Ferraro gestured for him to sit back down and walked over to him. Ferraro undressed quickly and got into the same tub.

Trussi kept his voice low. "So, what did you find out?"

"I went to the marketplace. Everyone was buzzing around and talking about how the queen had 'visited' the town. When I went to the market, her coach was already gone, and several people said they saw her leaving town. Once I heard that I came straight back." Ferraro leaned back, immersing himself in hot water as Remo had done.

Trussi got upset. "So, that's it? You didn't check to ensure she wasn't staying at one of the inns? Some people could lie because they want something to brag about."

"No, I didn't check. Look, the queen's coach was gone. That, I did check. And, besides, she is the queen! She isn't going to stay in a lowly inn with a bunch of peasants!! Everyone who saw her leave said she headed north towards the castle. Trust me. She is gone." Trussi nodded his head absentmindedly but was still a bit worried. Ferraro placed a hand on Trussi's shoulder.

"Trussi, I wouldn't suggest staying if I thought it would endanger any of us. She is gone, okay?"

Trussi nodded again and looked at the others. They were all exhausted, and this was the first time they had been warm in days. He could tell they needed a good rest.

"Okay, we'll stay for the night. But we are leaving first thing in the morning. We are no longer heading north. From here on out, we are traveling east." Ferraro smiled and nodded in agreement. He leaned back again, engulfing himself in the fantastic hot bathwater.

CH. 15   MAKING DUE

After their hot baths and a meal, everyone went to bed, falling asleep quickly. Everyone, that is, except for Trussi. His nerves were still too rattled to sleep. Sitting by the window, he watched for signs of trouble. Hours passed, but everything was still quiet and calm. As the night continued, his eyes grew heavy, and sleep finally took hold.

His dream felt deep. So deep that it nearly felt like he was falling.... Yes, he was falling! And, as he was falling, he could see glowing green eyes in the dark looming in the distance. They were looking at him, and he wanted to get as far away from them as possible. They were staring, not just at him, but through him, as if they were searching his soul. They started to get closer. He had to get away!!

The morning sun shining in his eyes woke Trussi from his deep sleep. He had fallen asleep by the window and raised his head. He grimaced and looked over at the beds. He discovered everyone else was getting up and starting to pack. Trussi shook his head, trying to get the remnants of the dream out of his head.

Once up, he packed with the others, and they all headed out to the market. Once everyone fully restocked their water and food supplies, the group headed east. This road quickly turned into a dirt road though it appeared well-maintained. As they were walking, Trussi began to feel less stressed.

'The more space between the queen and me, the better.' he thought.

Over the next five days, the weather varied between sunny and warm to rainy and cold and slightly warm. On the sixth day, they arrived at a small village. The market was small, but they were able to restock their supplies. Trussi knew this would be their last town on their trek, so he ensured everyone had extra food supplies.

Their journey would continue to the east. However, from this small town, no roads were going east, just thick woods. Trussi and Ferraro consulted the map occasionally. The group found the woods an arduous trek, and everyone traveled much slower. That night, they made camp and got a big campfire going. Trussi was grateful to have a fire as he and the others had heard the howling of wolves in the distance. They took rotations, ensuring that someone kept watch at all times, and the fire continued burning throughout the night.

Trussi awoke in the morning, glad to find everyone intact. They continued their way east, slowly and carefully. Everyone always kept a watchful eye out for any signs of wolves. Luckily, no one ever saw them. After another three days of traveling, they came upon a river. The area where Trussi wanted to go was located somewhere up past the river. So, instead of crossing, they followed it upstream for a few days more until it changed direction and they could continue their eastward journey.

After another six long, arduous days, they encountered a small clearing. Trussi checked his book, making sure the mountains in the distance, and everything else that was here, matched the descriptions perfectly. And there was even a small creek nearby! 'This will be perfect for the vegetable and herb garden I want to plant!' Trussi thought, already making plans.

"This is it!!" Trussi announced. "This is where we will build our new home. And look!" Trussi pointed to the closest mountain.

"That is where we'll mine and find our treasure!" he said excitedly.

Everyone was too exhausted to show enthusiasm as they camped for the night. There was still a nightly watch rotation, though the sounds of the wolves had not been present for several days. Trussi took the first watch. The new delight and joy caused him to be wide awake. He had already searched the area and picked out which trees he wanted to start using to construct their home. Trussi knew that as the weather was cooling down, they would need to build a shelter quickly. Not only that, but they would also need to stock up on firewood and food to survive the cold of the coming winter.

Trussi sighed. No one would even start thinking about mining until next spring. Everyone would be far too busy getting everything ready before winter sets in. Even when spring comes, he would need to restock supplies and set up planter boxes to get the vegetable seeds growing. Much needed to be done, so spring mining may be impossible and would likely start in summer. He sighed again. He wasn't typically a patient person. 'Mining will just have to wait,' he thought disappointedly.

In the morning, they wasted no time. Everyone that had an axe started chopping down trees under Trussi's guidance. They wouldn't have time to build an elaborate house, so a basic box-shaped shelter with a fireplace would have to do for now. Luckily, the creek nearby had many round stones and clay, the perfect foundation for building the fireplace they would need. Just like any structure, they started from the ground up. Progress was painfully slow, as the day was cold and overcast with gray clouds. Despite it going slow, Trussi decided they had made good progress for their first day's work.

As they were eating dinner, Trussi took stock of their remaining food. He was glad he had purchased extra food at the last town, but it was only enough to last a few weeks more. He had already checked the creek, but it didn't appear to hold any fish.

The next day, while everyone was working on the shelter, Trussi sent Marco upstream and Dante downstream to look for a pond or any signs of fish. After several hours, they both returned with disappointing information. Neither found any ponds, larger bodies of water, or any signs of fish or other foods.

Trussi needed more options. He had never hunted before but couldn't see any other way to get food. That night, around the campfire, he brought the subject up.

"I think everyone already knows there is no food in this creek. We need to find a food source to survive the winter. The only thing I can think of is hunting for meat. I'm open to other ideas if anyone else has any." Trussi looked around. Ferraro looked like he had an idea.

"What about snares? We could use those to try to catch some food."

Trussi agreed. "Not a bad idea. Do you know how to make and set snares?"

Ferraro shook his head " I have seen others set them. But, I have never set them myself."

Disappointed, Trussi looked at the others. "Does anyone know how to set snares?" Everyone looked down at their feet or shook their heads. "Okay, so setting snares is out. We'll have to hunt. But, the thing is, I have never hunted before. Does anyone here have any hunting experience?"

Dante spoke up, pointing to himself, Marco, and Loris. "When we were at the carnival, we used to take long sticks and sharpen the ends, making spears. We would hunt and eat squirrels when we were desperate for food. But, other than that, we don't have any hunting experience."

Trussi sighed. "Thank you, but we need considerably more food than what squirrel meat would provide."

He sat there thinking. Then an idea came to him. He remembered his book. There was a description of how one of the characters got meat. 'It might work.' he thought excitedly and scrambled to get his book out of his travel bag. He searched through the pages until he got to the precise part.

"My book talks about how they dug a trap pit to catch animals for food." He looked at the others. "We can do the same! We'll dig a pit and use that to catch some food."

Everyone groaned their complaints.

Trussi didn't give up. "Look, I know you are tired. I am too. But I think this could work."

Doc piped in, "If it doesn't work, then we would have wasted valuable time and energy on..."

Trussi cut him off, irritated. "If it doesn't work, we will run out of food and starve. Does anyone else have a better idea?" No one replied, as no one else had any other suggestions.

"Then it's settled. Tomorrow we'll dig a trap pit and start catching some food!" Trussi tried to sound optimistic, but he had never done this before and wasn't sure he could pull it off. He leaned back, trying to fall asleep. He was feeling uneasy, which made it difficult. 'This is going to work. It just has to!' he thought, trying to comfort himself.

In the morning, while the rest of the group continued making the shelter, Trussi took Ferraro, Loris, and Dante to look for a game trail. Once they found one, they chose an area to begin. Since they already had experience making sharp spears, Trussi figured he could have them make wooden spikes while he and Ferraro started digging. They picked a narrow traffic area for animals, evident by the animal prints on the ground.

Once Trussi instructed Loris and Dante, he and Ferraro started digging with their shovels. It was a challenging dig, as many rocks and roots were present. Despite this, they continued their labor, only occasionally stopping to drink water and catch their breath.

Trussi decided the trapping pit needed to be big enough to catch any sizeable beast. Not only that, but it needs to be deep enough so that the animal would not be able to jump out. That is if the fall didn't kill it first. The bottom of the pit would be lined with the sharp wooden spikes Loris and Dante were making to ensure it would kill the animal instantly.

By the end of the day, they had dug only about half the pit, yet Trussi found it challenging to climb out. Trussi needed Loris and Dante to help him after deciding they would need to make a ladder to get in and out of the pit as it got deeper.

'Tomorrow's project.' he thought to himself.

The next day, Trussi had Ferraro help him make the strong ladder he needed. It didn't take long, and once completed, they resumed digging. While doing this, Dante and Loris continued making more spikes. Working fast, they finished the pit by the end of the day. Trussi placed the spears at the bottom, ensuring they were well-placed and secure. He then took lightweight branches with leaves and grasses to cover the pit. He wasn't sure what to leave as bait, so he left a trail of stale bread across the trap.

'I can always change the bait if it doesn't work.' Trussi thought.

He looked it over one last time and decided the pit appeared hidden. He didn't want anyone to fall into the pit accidentally, so he tied a blue sash on the trunk of a nearby tree to mark the area. Once they rejoined the rest of the group, Trussi showed everyone where the colored strap was to prevent anyone from accidentally falling into the dangerous pit.

The following day, they all continued working on the shelter for winter. Trussi checked the pit several times during the day, only to find the stale bread remained untouched. That night he could barely sleep. 'What if we don't catch anything? What do we do for food then?' he stressfully pondered.

Over the next several days, they all continued building the shelter and the fireplace. Trussi occasionally checked on the game trap, but it lay quiet and undisturbed each time. On the third day, Trussi changed the bait and tried some of their jerked meat instead. Just as he decided this, Remo approached him and started tugging his sleeve.

"What's going on? I've got work to do!" Trussi tried to brush him off, but Remo kept pulling at him. "Hey, Doc! Please tell your son I have work to do and don't have time to play games!"

Doc came over, looking at Remo. "He's not trying to play with you. I think he wants to show you something." Remo nodded emphatically and jetted off in the direction he had been pointing. Trussi became concerned immediately.

"Hey, Remo!! Not so fast! No one should go wandering out here alone!" Trussi panicked.

Trussi and Doc both ran after him. They didn't seem to go far when Remo suddenly stopped. There was a tree right in front of Remo, which looked different from the other trees around. Growing on the tree were some rounded, almost tear-drop-shaped sacks. Some were green, but others were more of a deeper violet hue. Trussi wondered if it might be some fruit. But what fruit ripens in the fall? Remo reached up, plucking a purplish one out of the tree, and before anyone could say anything, he took a big bite.

"No!! Don't eat that," Doc shouted. "We don't know what that is! It could be poisonous!"

Remo immediately spat out the bite in his mouth and looked sadly down at the remaining fruit in his hand. Trussi took it, looking it over. He had never seen this kind of fruit before. The fruit was soft with thin, fragile skin, and the lavender and rose-colored flesh inside had many seeds.

"Let's take this to the others. Maybe one of them knows what kind of fruit this is and whether or not it is safe to eat." Trussi picked a green-colored one and the partially eaten purplish one to take with them.

Once they reached the rest of the group, Trussi showed them the fruit Remo had found. Marco, Dante, and Loris seemed to recognize it. Just as he presented it, Loris snatched it from Trussi's hand.

"This is a fig!" He exclaimed. This was the first time Trussi could recall ever hearing Loris speak. He had wondered if Loris was mute like Remo, but hearing him speak clarified that suspicion.

"What's a fig? And is it safe to eat?" Trussi questioned expectantly.

Loris nodded his head while looking at the fruit. "A fig is a fruit, a very delicious fruit. Sometimes, in our travels with the carnival, we would come across a town with fig trees. The green ones aren't ripe yet, but the violet ones are. Fig trees will give fruit once or twice a year. It can be early or late fall if they give the fruit a second time."

"So, to clarify, it is safe to eat?" Trussi wanted to be very sure he understood.

Loris nodded his head again and plopped the half-eaten fruit into his mouth. He chewed while smiling. "You don't have to peel them, either. The skin is edible too."

After seeing this, everyone dropped what they had in their hands and ran over to the fig tree. They all started picking the purple figs and devouring them. Trussi had never tasted anything quite like it. It was indeed very delicious. Once everyone had eaten their fill, Trussi wondered how a lone fig tree would grow in the woods.

"How do you suppose this tree got here? There aren't any other fig trees around here. Do you think someone could have planted it?"

"Perhaps a bird had eaten a fig. Then, as it flew, its droppings would have some fruit seeds. That's the only thing I would think about how a tree like this got here." Dante suggested.

"Sometimes, we would come across a tree that seemed out of place in our travels. A tree that didn't belong. When I asked about it, the response was always the same. An animal or a bird was likely the reason. They will eat the fruit, fly far away, and deposit the seeds as they leave their droppings."

Trussi eyed the fig tree. There were no other trees around like it. "Well, I suppose that's possible."

He scratched his head, wondering why he had never heard of this. Trussi then thought of the trap pit. He still needed to check it today. 'Perhaps this fig fruit would be better bait than stale bread,' he thought, picking some to take with him. Everyone resumed working on the shelter as Trussi took Remo to the pit.

"Good find, Remo." Trussi patted Remo on the back. "I just wanted to tell you that I am very proud of you for finding us some food." Remo smiled broadly and puffed out his chest, showing he was proud of himself too.

As they approached the pit, Trussi could tell something was off. He grabbed Remo by the arm, stopping him in mid-step. The branch coverings appeared broken, as if something had fallen through.

Trussi's voice was low and quiet. "Remo, you stay here. Let me look first to make sure it's safe." It could be perilous if the animal were still alive or possibly injured. Remo nodded, and Trussi stepped forward slowly and quietly.

He slowly approached the pit, peeking over the edge. Inside the cavity, he saw a wild boar. It was bloody and lying on its side with several spears sticking out. It was undoubtedly dead. Trussi sighed in relief, backed up from the pit, and walked over to Remo.

"It's a wild boar!" He proclaimed excitedly. "Let's go get the others. I'm going to need help getting it out of there!" They hurried back and got the rest of the group to help.

It took all seven of them, but they could finally lift the boar out of the pit. Once back at camp, Trussi and Ferraro prepared the boar for dinner. Trussi then stretched out the hide to dry in the sun. It was getting late and dark by the time a small fire was going, and they were able to start slowly roasting the whole boar.

"This won't be ready for dinner tonight," Doc sighed, "though I look forward to eating this tomorrow." Everyone else spoke up in excited agreement.

Doc looked away from the fire and turned towards Trussi. "Trussi, I want to apologize to you. When you suggested making this game pit, I wasn't supportive. I was wrong, and I am glad you didn't listen to me."

Trussi shook his head. He didn't want an apology from anyone. Before Trussi could say or refuse him, Doc held up his hand and continued.

"Everything you have done, leading us here, finding a way to get food, has all worked out despite some small setbacks. It has been an amazing adventure, even better than I had hoped." He paused, looking for the right words. "What I am trying to say is thank you. Thank you for allowing my son and me to join you on this great adventure."

Everyone nodded in agreement and started expressing their gratitude as well. Trussi felt embarrassed and awkward as it felt odd getting so much praise. He wanted to divert some attention, so he pointed to Remo.

"Don't forget! It was Remo who found the fig tree today." A round of cheers and gratitude exclaimed from everyone towards Remo.

The following day, Trussi took Marco and Loris back to the pit. They needed to make new spikes to replace the broken ones. Once securely in place, Trussi covered the hole like before, only this time, he placed several figs across the top as bait.

They resumed working on the shelter, which was coming along well. That night, they all ate roasted boar meat along with fresh figs. The meat was very tender and tasted amazing. As they were eating, Doc sat down next to Trussi. Doc pointed over to the boar skin, still stretched out for tanning.

"Hey, Trussi. I have a question for you. What do you plan on doing with that boar skin? I felt it, and it's pretty coarse. I can't imagine what you'd use that for."

Trussi laughed. "There's not much it is good for, that's true. But I will place it on the floor before the fireplace once the shelter is finished. Their skin is so strong that when sparks flick out of the fireplace, they are naturally extinguished on the hide without causing damage."

Trussi's grandmother had one when she was alive. He remembered how coarse it felt and how amazed he was at its sturdiness. Doc nodded and continued eating his meal. A fresh dinner filling their bellies felt terrific, and they all slept well that night.

Over the next several days, they continued working on the shelter, and Trussi would periodically check the game pit. After a few more days, they nearly finished the winter shelter. As Trussi rechecked the hole, he discovered it had caught a chamois. Trussi had always thought they looked strange, like a cross between a goat and an antelope.

He was glad to see the trap pit working well, as it would help sustain them for the winter. Later, on the same day, Trussi noticed that the first dusting of winter snow started to drift slowly. It wasn't enough to stick to the ground, but Trussi knew there would soon be more, a lot more.

CH. 16 UNEXPECTED VISITOR

Five Years Later

E veryone finished checking the game pits early in the morning. After the success of the first pit, they dug an additional two holes the following spring. They had caught nothing that day, so they headed towards the mountain mine to start the day's work. Trussi led the way, as usual, making their way through the woods. It was late spring, and the flowers were still blooming, making the forest floor colorful. The walk was calm and peaceful, and Trussi loved it.

It took the group nearly an hour to stroll to the mine entrance. Once there, Trussi was always the first to enter. He would often take his pickaxe and, in the areas of a fresh dig, would start dragging it behind him like it was heavy. Other times he would gently scrape it against the walls as he walked by.

Trussi had learned to do this occasionally, so as they dug into the mountain, he wasn't the only one to find gold and jewels. He also discovered that the amount of gold and gems the pickaxe would produce depended on how hard he struck. Gentle light touches made very little, while firmer and harder strikes would make much larger treasures.

Trussi would also often take a second pickaxe to mine dirt and rocks without having an overabundance of treasure before him after every swing. Also, every day he rotated spaces with one of the other dwarves, allowing someone else to find gold or jewels in the area Trussi had just left. Trussi did not find these tasks to be tedious or monotonous. Instead, he rather enjoyed it. Everyone was finding treasure which kept everyone's morale up. Of course, Ferraro knew what Trussi was doing. And, when they had first started mining, he had assisted Trussi in coming up with different ways to help ensure everyone at some time or another was finding gold and gems. Toward the end of the workday, they removed debris and dirt from the mine, dumping it over the cliff's edge. After collecting the riches they had mined for that day, everyone headed home. As they walked, they often told jokes or told stories about how they wanted to use their share of the riches.

Once they reached home and once inside, they would go directly to the fireplace. They had built a secret hidden door under the boar-skin rug, and when moved, a concealed door opened to steps that descended to a small hidden room. This room is where they stored their treasure. As everyone placed their daily haul into the storage room, Trussi took stock of how much they had. He knew this was probably their last year of mining. Trussi sighed, recalling the previous five years. He had loved every part of it, and the thought of leaving was bittersweet. Still, he missed Baccio, and the idea of seeing him again put a smile on his face.

Once everyone put the gold and gems away, Trussi and Marco rechecked the trapping pits. Luckily, one of the pits had caught a small red deer. The two brought it back to the house and prepared it for dinner. Everyone had their specific tasks, getting everything ready. The shelter improved significantly over the years and was now a modest cottage. They had even added an upstairs room with proper sleeping beds.

The only thing that initially needed to be added to their home was a large pot for making stew. That was remedied a few years back when five of them journeyed to the last town they had visited. Two of them remained behind to tend the garden and game pits.

Once the group reached the town, they purchased basic supplies, folk flutes, a mandolin, and a large cooking pot. It was a long journey there and an even longer journey carrying everything back. But, it had been worth it. They used the cooking pot quite a bit and had stew most nights, especially when the vegetables from Trussi's garden were ripe and ready.

This night, after they finished dinner, everyone rested while Loris, Dante, and Marco played their musical instruments and sang. Sometimes Doc or Ferraro would join in and sing, or they would jump up and dance to the music. Trussi enjoyed watching, although he didn't sing or dance. However, he did clap and laugh along with everyone else. After all that, they slept until the sun rose the following day.

The next day started like usual. Everyone completed morning tasks such as checking the pits and tending the garden. Once finished, they headed over to the mine to start another day's work. Trussi noticed the late spring flowers were becoming sparser. Summer was nearly upon them.

Once there, Trussi entered the mine first and took out his enchanted pickaxe. Again, like so many times before, he gently scraped it along the walls as he got deeper into the mine. With everyone in position, they started swinging their pickaxes. For this kind of work, Trussi was using his regular pickaxe, digging deep with every swing. He liked the work and how it felt when he got tired. He even enjoyed shoveling the dirt and rocks, carrying them out of the mine. Concentrating on the job helped keep his mind occupied, and he preferred it when his mind didn't wander.

Everyone was in high spirits when, at about midday, someone started talking about the journey back to their hometown. It wasn't unexpected, but Trussi had hoped such talk would have begun in the late summer or fall rather than the springtime. He sighed, knowing the inevitable return to their hometown was closer than he had wanted it to be. Thinking about this grand adventure, Trussi realized he had done everything he had set out to do. He had traveled far across the land, braved the wilderness, and made good friends. He had also mined a mountain, gaining treasure for himself and all his friends.

The thought of leaving made Trussi feel like something was uncompleted. Somehow, he felt this adventure of his was unfinished. It was as if there was still something more he was supposed to do. He couldn't put his finger on it, but something kept him drawn here, almost like a yearning or a longing.

Again, everyone gathered all the gold and gems in the evening and headed home. The walk home was just like it always was. Everyone joked or talked about how they wanted to spend their part of the treasure. As they got near the house, something felt off. As Trussi looked closer, he saw smoke coming out of the fireplace. The hair on the back of his neck tingled as he didn't remember anyone having made a fire before they left.

Trussi stopped dead in his tracks. "Everyone, stop!" He didn't shout, but his voice was intense. Everyone stopped and looked at the cottage seeing the smoke rising from the chimney.

"Did anyone light a fire in the fireplace before we left?" Trussi questioned. Everyone shook their heads. Trussi, along with the rest of the group, backed up slowly away. Once out of sight, they huddled together.

Marco looked concerned. "What's going on, guys? Who's here?" Everyone was bewildered. No one knew what was happening. "Maybe someone is here to steal our treasure!" Dante spouted.

Trussi shook his head. "No one knows where we are. Let alone what we are doing here. That doesn't make sense." He looked over, seeing Loris's face for the first time. Loris looked pale and appeared like he was going to faint.

"Do... do you think it is...." Loris gulped hard. "...it is the carnival coming to take us back."

Both Marco and Dante looked shocked and horrified at the same time. Loris started breathing hard as panic filled his face.

Finally, Trussi shook his head. "No, I don't think it is them. There are no caravans here and no horses. There is nothing around that makes me think it is them. Remember, they don't travel alone. And I do think that whoever is here is likely alone."

Trussi looked over at the three terrified orphans, placing a hand gently on Loris's shoulder. "Don't worry. Even if it were the carnival, we would never let them take you, no matter what." The three gathered their composure, and Loris started breathing normally again. Trussi had everyone huddle together.

"Okay. We need to figure out what is going on." Trussi didn't want to do anything rash, but he knew he wanted to keep everyone safe.

"I have an idea." Doc piped up. "How about we split into two groups and observe the house to see who is here and what is happening? Then we can meet back here before it gets dark."

"Great idea." Trussi and everyone else nodded in agreement.

Trussi took the lead. "I'll take Ferraro and Loris. We'll go to the south side of the house and observe. The rest of you go on the north side but stay out of sight."

They formed the two groups, and Trussi headed to the south side of the house. Staying out of sight was easy, but staying still proved difficult. Everyone was antsy, and nothing was happening. There were no sounds, no voices, and no movement. Trussi sighed. Staring at a house that appeared empty was boring, and he had a hard time not letting his mind wander. To keep his focus, Trussi tried to listen intently towards the house. Unfortunately, he heard nothing to indicate that someone was inside.

Trussi sighed. 'What if someone lit the fireplace before we left, and then they just forgot?' he thought, not convincing himself of the lie. He shook his head. 'No, that's not right. I would have seen the fireplace smoking as we left. There was nothing there this morning. Nothing!'

Trussi shifted where he was huddled and tried to remain quiet without letting his feet fall asleep. Time crept painfully slowly with no movement within the cottage at all. Trussi finally took his group back to the meeting place to see if the others had seen or heard something. Unfortunately, they discovered the other group had no luck seeing or hearing anything.

"Okay. So we'll have to think of something else." Trussi stated flatly.

After a while of discussion, Trussi had another idea. "How about this? I suspect there are only one or two people here. They would be noisier if there were a larger group, and we would have heard or seen something." Everyone nodded in agreement. "So, I think it is best to address this head-on."

Doc immediately looked concerned and interjected, "Just exactly what are you saying?"

"I think we need to go inside, see who is here, and find out what they want. And, if they want trouble, we'll be ready for them." Trussi pointed to the horizon. "It is going to be dark soon. We don't have any of our camping or survival supplies with us. I am unsure if we could survive without the necessities if we leave now. I'm open to other suggestions if anyone else has a better idea." Everyone shook their heads.

"Then we need to get ready. Everyone get your ax, pickaxe, or knives if you've got them. We're going to go in and take back our home!" Trussi sounded confident, but on the inside, he was terrified.

'What if this is a trap? There may be more than just one or two persons in there. What if there wasn't just a regular person inside? What if it was the queen in there?' The idea of seeing the queen again sent chills down his spine that made him shiver. Everyone got ready. Doc, Marco, and Loris had axes, while Dante and Remo had knives. Trussi was the only one armed with a pickaxe. It was the only thing he had on him at this moment he could use as a weapon.

Everyone approached the house slowly. Trussi looked again for any movement or sound, but everything within the house remained still. When they reached the front door, Trussi pushed it open slowly. Peeking inside, Trussi could see no sounds or signs of movement.

As he stepped inside, he suddenly heard a sneeze from behind him. Trussi turned with a start and instantly became upset at Dante for startling himself and the whole group. Once his heart stopped beating frantically, Trussi took several slow steps into the house. He glanced over at the fireplace. Indeed, the fire was going, but the odd thing about it was the cooking pot. It was over the fire, and looked like dinner was stewing inside.

Trussi walked closer. After a few steps, he could smell the aroma of potato stew. It smelled so good, and Trussi was tempted to taste it as he approached. He realized he was reaching for the spoon when he stopped himself. Trussi pushed the idea of tasting the stew out of his head. His stomach grumbled up at him, objecting to this rejection. 'This could be a witch's brew! It could be poisoned!' he thought.

Turning to the group, Trussi pointed to the pot and whispered, "No one takes a single bite until we know what is going on!" Unfortunately, no one else was paying attention. They weren't even behind him anymore! Everyone was scattered around the room, looking at different things.

"Look!!" Doc said, surprised. "Our dishes! Someone cleaned them and put them away too!" Everyone looked over at him, gasping about the dishes. Someone mentioned that the ground had been swept. Everyone then marveled at the floor after that. Trussi rolled his eyes. None of this mattered. Trussi snapped his fingers, trying to get their attention without shouting. Everyone looked at him.

"We need to check the other rooms to find out who is here!" Everyone nodded and gathered themselves up. Slowly, Trussi and the group thoroughly searched each room in the cottage. Strangely, they found each room empty. They gathered up again, and Trussi realized the only rooms they still needed to search were the hidden treasure room and the upstairs bedroom. Ferraro uncovered the secret door under the boar-skin rug. Trussi went down first, slowly, and everyone followed behind him. Once they reached the bottom, Trussi let out a sigh of relief. Everything was untouched and in its proper place. No one had been down here.

They went back up and re-covered the secret door. Trussi gathered everyone up again. "Okay. Whoever is here is surely in the upstairs bedroom." He swallowed hard. "I think someone needs to go upstairs and drive them down."

After saying this, Trussi thought about the queen again, about how her eyes glowed. And how she had turned, looking directly at him at the market, and then started walking towards him. Trussi shuddered at this memory and cringed as he remembered how he couldn't move. He immediately decided she wouldn't get whatever it was she came for. Especially after what he saw her do in the alleyway. No, he would end her first and stop her no matter what it took.

As everyone was figuring out who should go up, Trussi went ahead and volunteered himself.

"I'll go up by myself. I'll see who is here and bring them downstairs. If they mean harm to us and attack me, then I want all of you to leave immediately."

Ferraro shook his head. "No. You are not going up there alone, and there is no way we are leaving without you!" Everyone tried to argue along with Ferraro. But Trussi couldn't bear the idea of anything terrible happening to them. He put his hands up.

"This is not up for debate! I am the only one going up there. The rest of you stay down here and be ready. If the intruder attacks me, then I don't want the rest of you to be in danger. You are to leave! Is that clear?" Trussi sounded angry and forceful despite the fear swelling up inside him.

The rest of the group remained silent. The looks on their faces were solemn and grim. Trussi grabbed a large knife from the kitchen, putting his pickaxe down. A much better weapon, he decided. Turning around, he saw the looks on everyone's faces again. They were all concerned and scared. Trussi pushed past all of them before anyone could argue any further. His grasp on the knife tightened as he approached the bottom of the stairs. Looking up, he could see the door at the top stairs was shut, and no sounds were coming from within.

Taking a deep breath, he started walking up the stairs slowly. Luckily, the wooden stairs had been built well and weren't creaky. Still, Trussi needed time to think about what he would do when he found the queen, so every step was precise and slow.

Strega's warning echoed in his mind as he made his way up. 'Beware the queen!'

Trussi swallowed hard. 'I have to be quick,' he decided, 'before her magic takes hold and I cannot move.' Finally, he reached the top of the stairs. Trussi could feel his heart pounding in his chest, and his hands started to tremble from his anticipation. 'Should I open the door quickly, bursting in and taking her by surprise? Or should I open it slowly and quietly to see where she is before I enter?'

He grabbed the door handle, pausing in thought. He didn't like either option as they both created opportunities for Trussi to be vulnerable to an attack. After careful consideration, he made a decision. Sucking in a deep breath, Trussi pushed the door open, bursting into the room. Once in there, he nearly thought the space was empty. But, as he looked it over quickly, he saw a significant figure lying across three beds.

The figure was covered in blankets, and Trussi could see the person underneath was stirring. If this were the queen, now would be the best time to strike! Trussi jetted over to the beds. He clasped the knife with both hands and raised it high. The figure under the bed stirred some more. 'Now! This has to be now!'

He closed his eyes, readying himself to plunge the knife down. Just as he started to bring the knife down, a sudden thought occurred, and he stopped midair. The queen would never sleep in some peasant's bed, let alone three dwarves' beds! As he lowered his knife, the figure under the blankets stretched and moaned as she awakened.

Trussi could see the blankets move as the person sat up. When the coverings fell away, Trussi could see; indeed, she was not the queen! Instead, before him was the most beautiful girl Trussi had ever seen! Her lips were blood red, her hair was black as ebony, and her skin was pale like freshly fallen snow.

The beautiful girl looked horrified at Trussi when she saw him standing close to her holding a knife. Trussi slowly put the knife down and placed his palms in the air.

"I won't hurt you." He said as calmly as he could. "I am sorry that

I startled you, but we didn't know who was in our house and if they meant us harm."

The girl slowly relaxed and took a deep breath. "Thank goodness." She sighed, her voice sounding soft and sweet.

He was relieved this girl was not the queen. But now, he was filled with questions. Trussi needed to get some answers and asked as politely as they could. "Who are you, and why are you in our house?"

Before the girl could answer, Trussi heard a sound from behind him. Looking back, he could see Ferraro poking his head through the open door with a knife ready in hand.

"Trussi, it's too quiet in here. Is everything okay?" Saying this, Ferraro looked past Trussi and noticed the girl. "My goodness!" he exclaimed in surprise and dropped his knife.

Just then, the girl giggled. "Everything in this house was so small, and I was sure children lived here! But you're not children. You're dwarves!" Her smile was so beautiful and delightful that Trussi couldn't help but smile along with her. What was wrong with him? Once Trussi realized he was smiling, he turned away, shaking his head.

There was an awkward pause, so Ferraro cleared his throat. "I don't mean to make this awkward, but, my dear, just who are you, and why are you here?"

The girl stopped smiling and looked sad. She hesitated before answering, "I'm Snow white." She paused momentarily and then gasped, "Oh, the soup! It'll burn!!" Snow white hopped out of the beds, ran out of the room, and started down the stairs.

Ferraro and Trussi followed after her. "Wait..." they called out, but the girl was quick and was downstairs before she could hear them. She immediately ran to the boiling pot and started stirring and smelling the contents.

"Good!" She said enthusiastically. "It hasn't burned." The rest of the dwarves looked shocked upon seeing such a lovely girl in their house. They stood still and gaped at her with open mouths. Trussi and Ferraro quickly descended the stairs, joining the rest of the group, who appeared confused and unsure of what to do.

Snow White continued concentrating on her soup, unaware of her audience. Trussi finally cleared his throat. "So you said your name is Snow White?" he asked. Nodding, she looked up and saw the group of dwarves watching her. Smiling, she turned towards everyone.

As she curtsied, Snow White responded, "Yes. It is a pleasure to meet you all. May I ask your names?" Her soft voice sounded pleasant and lovely. Trussi could see everyone's concerns melt away as she spoke.

All the dwarves introduced themselves, with Trussi being the last to say his name. Once everyone introduced themselves, the dwarves, except for Trussi, started exclaiming questions. "How did you get here?" "Where did you come from?" "Did you travel far?" "Is there anyone with you?" When Snow White opened her mouth to answer a question, The group threw even more questions at her. "You're not a witch, are you?" "Are you married?" "Is that witch's brew?" Trussi decided it was enough. If they were to learn anything about why the girl was here, she would have to be allowed to talk.

"Enough!" he shouted above the bustling questions. Everyone quieted down.

"She can't answer anyone's questions if no one will let her speak." He gestured towards Snow White. "Now then, please explain where you came from and how you found our cottage while lost in the woods?"

She smiled then. "Of course, I would be glad to explain ... But first, I think we should eat! Dinner is ready, and I am famished. There should be enough for everyone." Glancing around at the group, her smile deepened. "You don't have to worry, I am not a witch, and this is not a witch's brew. If you are concerned, I would happily eat the first bowl to show you it is perfectly safe."

With that, Snow White filled a bowl and, after sitting at the table, started to eat. Everyone else became excited and began to fill bowls for themselves. They all sat down politely as close to Snow White as possible. She seemed to barely notice, though, eating her soup slowly and gracefully.

Trussi didn't like that no one had asked or consulted with him before doing this. What if this was some trick? He didn't fill a bowl as his suspicion made him question whether it was safe. She may not be the queen, but the queen could have sent her. Still, he sat at the table as the others began to eat. Everyone seemed to enjoy the meal, and Trussi could feel his stomach grumbling unhappily.

Once everyone's bowls were empty, all eyes were on Snow White. Realizing everyone was waiting for her to start, she began her tale. "You already know that I am Snow White. My father was king until he passed away ...."

Dante interrupted. "So that means you are the princess!!" he exclaimed. Everyone let out astounded comments that they had a princess in their home.

She nodded 'yes' and continued. "After my father died, my stepmother, the queen, kept me as a servant in the castle." She paused for a moment and furrowed her brows in thought. "Just the other day, she was being unusually nice to me. She gave me a clean and lovely dress and sent me to the edge of the woods to fetch flowers.

"I thought she was getting ready to marry me in some faraway land. But, as I picked flowers, the huntsman who chaperoned me pulled out a knife to kill me."

Everyone at the table gasped and expressed their disgust at the man.

"But he stopped and begged for forgiveness. He said the queen sent him to kill me!" Snow White looked sad as she said this, and tears started forming in the corners of her perfect almond-shaped eyes. Her long eyelashes were batting as she tried to prevent the tears from flowing.

Even more gasps and disgusted comments flooded the table.

"He told me the queen was jealous, and I needed to run away and never come back." She paused again as a solitary tear slid down one of her lovely rosy cheeks. "So I ran. I ran into the woods. I did not know where I was going. I just kept running and running. Soon, I became utterly lost and ended up lying inside a hollow log for the night. I couldn't sleep much as I was too scared and freezing.

"The next day, I didn't know which direction I came from, so I just started walking. After a very long two days, I found this cottage. I was scared, but I needed food and rest. I was waiting for someone to answer when I knocked on the door, but no answer came. The door was unlocked, so I went inside. I could see all the furniture was small, and I assumed children lived in this house. Since no one was home, I started preparing supper and cleaning the house. I was hoping the children that did live here would let me stay...."

"We are certainly not children." Ferraro interrupted politely.

Snow white smiled brightly and giggled again. "Certainly you are not!!"

The whole table broke out in laughter. Trussi couldn't see the humor in what was said. Instead, he was too focused on one of Snow White's first words. "Let me get this right. The queen is your stepmother. And she wants you dead?"

She looked at him. Her eyes were sad as she answered quietly. "Yes. That is correct."

Everyone again expressed how terrible the queen was. Trussi felt his stomach lurch. He was sure it would not have stayed in his stomach if he had eaten any of the stew. Thoughts of Strega and her warnings to stay away from queen Regina echoed within his head. If Regina was indeed after Snow White, then the likelihood of her showing up was very high. Trussi shuddered at the thought of seeing her again. The memory of her glowing green eyes was permanently burned into his mind, and he had no desire to be in her presence ever again.

Trussi wasn't sure who pipped in that Snow White was welcome to stay, but the moment it was said, the girl jumped up with delight. "Oh, thank you! Thank you!! I am certain the queen would never find me here!"

It all happened so fast. Everyone seemed to agree, and Trussi felt this decision was too hasty. No one had discussed anything or had even asked him his opinion! He was sure he should object but couldn't find the words. He did indeed feel sorry for Snow White. She was innocent of any wrongdoings and didn't deserve to be murdered out of jealousy. Where would she go if he were to cast her out? He sighed, thinking to himself. 'What have we got ourselves into? Do they not see the danger we are putting ourselves in by helping this girl?'

Ferraro placed a hand on Trussi's shoulder just then. "Are you doing okay? You look like you need some fresh air. Why don't we step outside so we can speak privately?"

Trussi stood up, finding that his knees felt weak. Everyone was busy asking Snow white questions and didn't appear to notice Trussi and Ferraro excused themselves from the table. Once outside, Trussi took several deep, slow breaths. The fresh air indeed felt calming.

"I don't like this." Ferraro's voice was calm but very concerned.

Trussi agreed. "Neither do I." He paused for a moment, sucking in a deep breath.

Ferraro continued, "I don't like anything about this situation. This whole situation with you, this princess, and your relation to the queen! It almost feels like some setup!"

Trussi looked away. The mere mention of the queen made his stomach knot up.

Ferraro ran his hands nervously through his hair as he continued to speak. "It's not that I don't want to help the poor girl. But with her staying here, it puts us all in danger. Does no one see that?!" He shook his head and closed his eyes.

"I couldn't live with myself if any of them were hurt or worse ..." Ferraro couldn't complete the sentence.

Trussi agreed, "And neither could I. So, what would you have us do then? Cast the poor girl back out into the woods alone? Or perhaps take her to the next town and dump her off? You know, if we do either of those options, the queen is sure to find her."

Trussi's eyes furrowed at the memory of seeing the queen in the alleyway. She had killed that young girl without hesitation and would do so again. Trussi sighed. He needed time to think. He didn't want everyone he cared about to be put in danger. Sitting down right where he stood, Trussi cupped his face in his hands. There didn't seem to be any good options. Ferraro stood beside him, racking his brain, trying to think of what to do as well.

Trussi then remembered what the queen had said to the girl in the alleyway just before she had her killed. Trussi stood up quickly. "I think I have an idea!! Do you remember what I told you about what I saw in the alleyway with the queen?" Ferraro nodded, and Trussi continued. "She said there could only be one fairest in the land. What if Snow White was no longer in her land?"

A smile quickly formed on Ferraro's face. "Oh my goodness, Trussi, that's genius!" Pausing a moment, he realized a minor flaw in that plan. "We'll need to check the map to see where to go. If the nearest border is north, we must figure something else out." Trussi agreed with that idea.

"There is something more, Trussi. This will only work if you tell everyone the truth. The others need to know what you witnessed the queen doing in that alleyway with that girl." Trussi was about to object, but Ferraro cut him off.

"I don't expect you to disclose everything. We can keep the enchantment of your pickaxe between ourselves. But if we want to get Snow White to safety, the others will need to know just how dangerous the queen truly is."

Just then, the front door opened. Trussi and Ferraro turned, seeing Doc leave the cottage and approach them. "We were wondering where you had gone off to. Is everything okay?"

Ferraro replied, "Not really. There is something important we need to discuss later tonight with everyone."

Doc raised his eyebrows and nodded. "I'll let the others know." He paused momentarily, then continued, "Everyone has started playing music for Snow White." Though it wasn't a question, it felt like Doc was asking if they would join them.

Ferraro mustered up as much of a smile as he could. "Thank you. We will be in shortly."

CH. 17 THE RED APPLE

russi and Ferraro entered the house shortly after Doc. Trussi could already hear Loris, Dante, and Marco playing music on the flutes and mandolin. The lovely Snow White was sitting comfortably while joyfully clapping along. Everyone seemed to be happy and in high spirits.

Just as Trussi had approached the group, he saw Remo walk over to the princess and offer his hand. She smiled as she took it, and the two started dancing together. Remo had the biggest smile that Trussi had ever seen on his face.

Doc and Ferraro sat close by and joined in with the clapping. Trussi did too, but initially found no joy in the music. Thoughts of the queen still weighed heavily on his mind. After a while, Doc joined in and started singing as well. Shortly after, he also danced with the princess.

Someone started laughing, and without realizing it, Trussi smiled and laughed also. It felt good to focus on something else, and he began to enjoy himself. Before he knew it, Trussi stood up, joining the dance with everyone. Loris, Dante, and Marco also took turns dancing, each enjoying the lighthearted fun.

After a while, when everyone was tired, they all bid Snow White goodnight. She offered to sleep downstairs so they could take the beds upstairs. Everyone dismissed her offer, saying they would be fine sleeping downstairs. She smiled gratefully and thanked them for their generosity. Heading upstairs, she glanced back at the group and smiled before shutting the door behind her.

Ferraro then collected his map and reviewed it with Trussi. Unfortunately, the closest border outside these lands was northwest, towards the queen's castle. Upon further review, Trussi could see that to the south of their dwarf town, the border of the kingdom ended, but so did the land. Luckily according to the map, there was a mainland to another continent not far. Seeing this, Trussi pointed it out to Ferraro. "Look, this is where the queen's kingdom ends. It looks like a fishing town along the coast, which is south of our village. If we could get Snow White there, I bet we could find a trading ship to take her to this other land. If we can do that, Snow White would be outside the queen's borders and on a different continent altogether."

Ferraro looked over the map carefully. It was a good idea. However, there would be a great deal of travel. After reviewing every possible direction, Ferraro finally agreed. "I cannot find a better route to take us out of these borders. However, I wouldn't say I like how far we have to travel. Even after we get her to our village, there will still be a long journey ahead." He rubbed his head in thought. And after reviewing the map one last time, he could not find a better solution and put the map away. e

Ferraro gathered everyone around for the upcoming conversation. Trussi sighed to himself. He spoke clearly but quietly, as he didn't want to disturb the sleeping princess. He told them how he had met Strega, how she told him of his family's relation to the queen, and her warnings about the queen.

Trussi then told them how he had seen the queen in one of the towns they had visited and what he saw her do to the girl in the alleyway. No one interrupted, and they all listened intently to everything he said. Once finished, Trussi could see several of them had some questions.

Loris piped in first, "Why didn't you tell us what happened in the town with the queen? Why would you keep that from us?"

Trussi shrugged his shoulders. "There was already a lot on everyone's minds. We were trying to avoid the carnival, and I didn't want to add to everyone's stress."

Doc leaned forward and asked, "So why are you telling us this now?"

Trussi swallowed hard. "Because you deserve to know the truth. And Ferraro and I don't think Snow White is safe here. If the queen wants her dead, she will find and end her. This situation will put her and us all in danger." Everyone became instantly upset and started arguing. Trussi placed his hand up, quieting everyone down.

"We have a plan. Ferraro and I believe taking Snow White out of the queen's land is the best way to keep her safe. We plan to return to our home village and bring Snow White. From there, Snow White, Ferraro, and I will continue traveling south toward the ocean border. Once we reach the harbor, we can put her on a boat and send her overseas. She'll be out of reach of the queen and safe."

Everyone looked displeased, though no one said anything. After a short while, Doc finally spoke up. "I don't like the idea of you two traveling alone with Snow White. If what you said is true, your journey could be dangerous. You're going to need all the help you can get."

Trussi shook his head and was going to argue, but Dante spoke up before he could refute. "That's right! No way will we let you take on danger all by yourself. We are coming with you, all the way, until Snow White is safe and sound." Everyone nodded 'yes' or spoke their agreement.

Trussi huffed, trying to release some of his frustration. "Look. This is possibly dangerous. Someone could get hurt, and someone could get killed. I couldn't live with myself if anything like that happened."

Looking around, Trussi could see everyone's resolve. They would not agree to allow him and Ferraro to take on this burden alone, no matter what he said. He smiled, despite his frustration. He had true friends. Friends who would risk their lives to help protect one another.

"Fine. It's agreed. We will all stick together until Snow White is safely out of the queen's peril." Loris finalized.

Everyone appeared appeased, and they all settled down for the night. No beds were downstairs, so everyone had to make the best of it. Several lay in front of the fireplace while others huddled together using multiple skin rugs. Trussi ended up propping several table chairs together. He used his travel sack as a pillow to lay his head on. Despite his awkward position, he fell asleep quickly.

In the morning, they inform Snow White of the plan to take her out of the kingdom. At first, she seemed hesitant regarding the idea.

"I don't know. It is a very long journey. Are you sure there is no other way?" Snow White inquired.

Ferraro nodded, showing her his map. "The only other way would leave us traveling back to the castle and then continuing north from there."

She eyed the map, tenderly touching it as she made her way in every direction. After a short moment, she looked up and sighed. "I guess you are right. Though I wish there were a better way."

Trussi patted her hand, trying to comfort her. "Believe me. I wish there were too." She looked at him, batting her long lashes. He could see tears starting to form in her eyes. Seeing her so sad, Trussi could feel a tightening in his chest, and he wished he could ease her sorrow.

"Please, don't think of this like you are trying to escape danger. Try to think of this as an adventure." Trussi made sure to sound very optimistic.

She shook her head. "But when this is over, I'll be alone in a strange new place... What will I do then?" Several tears trickled down her cheek as she hung her head.

Doc came over and gently clasped her other hand. "Well, you know, my dear, I had no intention of returning to our hometown. My son and I would love to accompany you on this journey to the unknown. That is if you would like us to join you."

She looked up and, without hesitation, opened her arms and squeezed him in a warm, embracing hug. "Oh yes!" she exclaimed. "Thank you so much. I would love to have you and Remo accompany me." Snow White laughed loudly as she hugged him gratefully.

Trussi could see Doc blushing as the embrace ended. He even felt slightly jealous at the idea of Doc going on another adventure in a foreign land. 'Something new to search and explore would be grand.' he thought. Looking again at Snow White, he wasn't quite sure the jealousy he felt was really towards the adventure.

She turned toward the group and exclaimed. "You have all been so kind to me. Thank you so much for everything!"

The others also started blushing and responded, "It's nothing." "My pleasure." and "Glad to help." Trussi blushed, too, as she turned toward him with a smile.

He couldn't help but return her smile and said, "Glad that's settled. We should start packing for the long journey ahead immediately." With that, everyone started preparing for the long journey back to their hometown.

The next few days went by quickly. Deciding what they should bring and what should stay was relatively easy, and there were little to no arguments. Right away, Trussi found some supplies to make several travoises. These simple wooden load-bearing frames would need to carry some of the heavy treasure they had collected. Once the travois' were completed and the supplies were packed, Trussi briefly looked around one last time. They had everything they needed, and anything left in the cottage was put away neatly, just in case any of them were to return. They even left some of the treasure tucked away in the hidden room. There was too much to take, which would have bogged their journey.

Satisfied that everything was packed, Trussi shut the front door behind him. There was no lock, but no one was worried about thieves this far out in the woods. Despite feeling reluctant to leave, the thought of seeing Baccio again made him glad he was traveling home. As they started to head out, he glanced back at the cottage one last time and smiled.

The nearest town would take multiple days, and Trussi was initially worried about traveling with a girl. He figured it would be more challenging as he wondered how well she would fare on the arduous journey. But, as the day progressed, he found she never complained and could easily keep up with everyone. She would even sing songs along the way, making the expedition seem less laborious. Camping with her was also very pleasant as she was good at building a fire and accommodating with packing in the mornings.

Once they had just reached the first town, Trussi gathered everyone before entering. "I don't think having Snow White enter the town is wise. We don't want to risk anyone recognizing her." Pausing a moment, he looked at Snow White's clothes. What was once a lovely dress was tattered and torn in many places. It had not fared well from when she had scrambled through the woods.

"While we are in town, we can pick up some new clothes for you as well," Trussi told her.

She smiled big at him, saying, "Thank you! That would be just wonderful!"

Trussi could have sworn he felt his heart flutter just a little. Looking away, he directed the rest of the group.

"Doc, you and Remo stay with her and remain out of sight. We will gather the necessary supplies and meet back here soon." Everyone agreed, and Trussi headed out with Ferraro, Dante, Marco, and Loris.

The town was small, and so was the market. Everyone made sure to stay close together as they gathered supplies quickly. Luckily, finding supplies was easy. Once fully stocked, Trussi started looking for a dress. He found and purchased several modest dresses, as he didn't want anything flashy to avoid attracting attention. He also bought travel boots for the girl, as the shoes she was already wearing were clearly not meant for traveling.

Satisfied with everything, they went back to meet with the others. After Snow White changed privately, they all walked around the outskirts of town, keeping out of sight. Once they came across the familiar cobblestone road, they followed it, heading west. The trek down the road was considerably easier than trudging through the woods, and they were all grateful they no longer needed to walk through foliage. Everyone traveled well over the next few days as the weather was favorable.

Heavy spring rain soon came, and they decided to stay at the next inn for the night. The town they approached was where Trussi had seen the queen murder the young girl. He was anxious upon entering but was quickly comforted by Ferraro. They decided to go to a smaller inn this time, and Trussi promptly paid for the rooms.

Several of them stayed outside with Snow White, keeping her out of view from the innkeeper. Once Trussi completed the payment, they all went up for the night as discreetly as possible, with the princess crouching down as much as possible to make it look like she was a dwarf. No one appeared to notice or care, and they stayed the night without any apparent issues.

In the morning, continuing on their way towards the south, Trussi was surprised everything was going so smoothly. Several more days passed, and they discovered they could easily avoid others on the road and stocked up on supplies without any issues. The closer he got to his hometown, the more relaxed he became.

'This is going to work!" he decided to himself. Along the way, Snow White was very helpful during their travels, never leaving anyone alone to take on a heavy task. Everyone seemed to enjoy having her journey with them, and Trussi noticed the others smiling and joking around considerably more because of her.

While traveling, when she wasn't singing, Snow White often spoke to Remo, who could only listen or nod his head. She also frequently talked to Trussi along the way, and he secretly looked forward to their chats. It reminded him of how Giada and he used to talk together. He usually avoided conversations about Giada, but with Snow White, it came effortlessly.

Feeling this way was odd, as he usually avoided conversations with females. The memory of Giada was still so painful, causing Trussi purposely never get close to any girl. Only after several more days with Snow White did he realize that talking with the girl didn't make him think of Giada less often. Instead, it just made her memory far less painful.

Trussi found that as the days passed, he enjoyed this girl's company and relished spending time with her. She was thoughtful, kind, and intelligent. She told him how she had secretly taught herself to read despite being forced into servitude. Trussi knew very few could read, making him respect and appreciate her even more.

The more she shared with him, the more he shared with her.

This was something he rarely did with others. Snow White also found it easy to talk with Trussi, and conversation flowed effortlessly between them. Snow White disclosed things close to her heart that she had never told anyone else.

Trussi also found that though he cared dearly for Remo, he would feel slightly jealous anytime she had conversations with him. Trussi made it a point to talk with her often, taking up much of her free time as possible. Time went by fast this way, talking about anything, and the days melted carelessly into each other.

Soon, the cobbled road turned into a dirt road, and all the dwarves knew they were close to reaching their hometown. Trussi could tell everyone was becoming more excited with anticipation. They followed the dirt road, checking the map when they reached several crossroads. Finally, they arrived at the only crossroads Trussi was familiar with and knew they were on the brink of their hometown.

Hastening with excitement, they reached the village quickly. Trussi could see the sun was touching the horizon as they arrived, and he knew it would be dark soon. The group headed to Ferraro's old house, knowing Baccio and his wife would be there. Trussi realized he hadn't even seen Baccio's child yet and wondered if the kid was a boy or a girl. Once they reached the house, Trussi knocked quickly on the door.

Baccio opened the door, looking Trussi straight in the eyes. Not even pausing, a large grin formed on their faces, and they embraced each other with tight-gripped hugs. Trussi didn't want to cry, and, despite his internal objections, his eyes flowed heavily with tears of joy. Baccio finally let go, wiping tears away from his own eyes.

"Please come in! All of you! I want to hear about all your travels!"

Before Trussi could say anything about Snow White, Baccio turned and pulled him inside. When they entered, Trussi was greeted by Baccio's wife, who was visibly pregnant again. She smiled as she greeted them and didn't appear startled or concerned when she welcomed the tall girl in their group.

Baccio called out two names, "Matteo and Emma, come out here! There are some people I'd like you to meet!" Trussi's eyes raised in surprise as he saw a boy and a girl, about five years of age, come out of a back room.

"My goodness, Baccio! You had twins?!"

Baccio smiled broadly, puffing out his chest with pride. He bent down to his kids and gestured towards Trussi. "Matteo and Emma, I want you to meet my brother, Trussi. He's the one I've been telling you about. The one who left to go on a grand adventure."

Both kids looked at him with wide eyes. Trussi tilted his head towards them. "It is very nice to meet you, Matteo and Emma." The two children giggled and then tackled him with hugs.

Ferraro cleared his throat. "Baccio, there is something we need to..."

Baccio cut him off. "And this is Ferraro!! He is the one who gave us this amazing house to live in!!" The two children then turned to Ferraro and tackled him as well. He tried to stop them but was unsuccessful. Laughter filled the room, and then Baccio noticed the unusually tall girl in his home.

"Trussi," he whispered, "may I ask who that girl is?"

Trussi placed his hand on Baccio's shoulder. "I will be glad to explain everything. However, there is much to tell."

Baccio nodded and instructed his wife to prepare dinner for the group. She happily nodded and began preparations. Snow White offered to help though Trussi wasn't sure how much help she would be, as she had to hunch over when she stood.

Baccio, Trussi, and Ferraro went to the backyard to speak while the others rested inside. Baccio hugged Ferraro just then, pulling Trussi in with him. They held this embrace for a while before Baccio let go, once more wiping his eyes.

"I was so worried. When you didn't come back after the second and third year..." Baccio's voice choked, and he swallowed hard. "...I was worried that I was never going to see you again."

Ferraro patted Baccio's shoulder. "Come now. You ought to know us better than that." But the look on Baccio's face showed his distress.

Trussi patted him on the other shoulder to reassure him.

"I'm sorry my journey and adventure took longer than expected, but, to tell you the truth, it isn't completely over yet."

Baccio raised his eyebrows. "I don't understand. You are home now. What more could there possibly be left to do!"

Trussi and Ferraro told him about their travels, finding the three enslaved orphans, and about Trussi meeting Strega. They didn't leave out the part where Strega enchanted his pickaxe, as Trussi felt that Baccio deserved to know the whole truth. At first, Baccio didn't believe him about the pickaxe. But, after Trussi demonstrated how it worked, Baccio became very quiet and listened intently to the rest of their tale.

They then told him how Trussi had seen the queen in the marketplace and again in the alleyway. It was there that he saw her have that young girl murdered. Lastly, they told him about Snow White showing up, how she was the princess, and that she was fleeing the queen who wanted to kill her.

After they finished, Baccio ran his hands through his hair. "That is quite a tale. If I didn't know you two or hadn't just seen what that pickaxe did, I wouldn't believe you." He shook his head, clearly unnerved at the tale just said to him.

Turning to Trussi, Baccio eyed him suspiciously. "There's something you haven't told me yet. You said your journey isn't completely over. What did you mean by that?"

Trussi looked away, "Well, we plan to continue traveling south tomorrow. We will travel until we reach the coast, where there is a fishing harbor. From there, we will find a boat heading to the next continent and buy passage for Snow White to get her beyond the queen's borders. She won't be alone as Doc and Remo have decided to go with her."

Letting out a deep breath, Trussi looked Baccio square in the eyes. "We will return after she has safely set sail. And, when I return, it will be for good."

Baccio nodded his head absent-mindedly, then looked down at the ground. "You just got here. I can't believe you're leaving first thing."

Ferraro spoke just then. "Well, it doesn't have to be first thing in the morning. We still need to stock up on supplies before we head out."

Baccio gave Trussi a partial smile. "Spending the morning together is better than not spending any time together."

Trussi smiled back. "Don't worry. When I return, we'll have plenty of time to catch up. We'll spend so much time together you'll be sick of me." Thinking momentarily, he suggested, "How about we go fishing tomorrow morning? It'll give the others time to gather what we'll need at the market. This way, it'll just be you and me."

"I would like that very much." Baccio smiled at the suggestion and gave Trussi one last embrace.

After that, they went back inside, re-joining the others. Everyone told stories about their journey or made jokes, keeping the ambiance optimistic. Dinner was ready within a short time, and everyone ate heartily.

Once everyone had eaten their fill, Trussi and Snow White stayed with Baccio while everyone else left to rest at the local inn. Snow White was too tall for just one bed, so Trussi pushed the two spare beds together for her. He decided to sleep near the hearth. The warmth of the cinders reminded Trussi of how much time spent his childhood reading by the fire in his grandmother's house. Thinking this made him want to get his book out to read, but he was too tired. He closed his eyes, and a deep, dreamless sleep found him quickly.

In the morning, Trussi looked around for Baccio. He couldn't find him in the house, so he stepped outside in the backyard. Baccio was there, fiddling with Trussi's pickaxe.

Seeing this, Trussi smiled. "I thought I told you it won't work for anyone but me."

Baccio nodded his head, smirked, and shrugged his shoulders. "I know. I couldn't help but try it anyway." He handed the pickaxe back to Trussi.

Trussi set it down. "Shouldn't we be going fishing?"

"I've already got the fishing gear." Baccio smiled broadly then.

Seeing they had everything they needed, Trussi set out for the pond with Baccio. Walking there was done with a relaxed, leisurely pace, and Trussi relished it. It felt nice talking and laughing as Baccio told him about the trouble his kids would cause. Hearing some of these stories, Trussi was glad to be home and looked forward to staying when he returned for good.

They set their lines in the pond, getting small nibbles occasionally but didn't catch anything. Neither minded, as they were too busy discussing what each other had experienced over the last few years to care about the fish. As the afternoon approached, Trussi groaned internally, knowing it was time to leave. This day had been fantastic, and he didn't want it to end.

Heading home, they again walked with a relaxed, unhurried pace. Once they reached home, Trussi paused before entering. The hair on the back of his neck stood on end. Something was wrong. Very wrong. The house was quiet when it should have been bustling with sounds from Baccio's wife, his kids, and Snow White.

"This doesn't feel right. Something's wrong." Baccio said as he reached the front door.

A look of horror spread across his face, and Baccio surged forward, calling out for his wife. Trussi hurried after him. Inside, the house was a mess. Tables were knocked over, and belongings were scattered and spilled over the floor. Trussi could hear children crying, and they both ran towards the sound. In the kitchen lay Snow White, unmoving with Baccio's wife close by. She was lying on the floor but conscious and was bleeding slightly from the side of her head. Both children clung to her apron and dress while crying.

Baccio ran to her." My dear, are you alright? What happened?!"

The moment Baccio ran to his wife, Trussi ran to Snow White. She didn't move as he clasped her shoulders. Her body was limp, and he could see she was not breathing. As he grabbed her, he saw a very red apple fall out of her hand with a large bite taken out of it. He recognized the apple the very moment he saw it. It was an apple from his grandmother's apple trees.

Realizing the queen would know about the apple trees struck him like lightning, and he nearly fell over. He then shook Snow White, trying to wake her, but she remained motionless. Turning to Baccio, Trussi could see his wife holding her head and telling Baccio she was okay.

She pointed towards the backyard. "The old lady..." She panted. "The old beggar lady came to sell apples. She gave Snow White one, and once she had a single bite, she fell over dead! The old lady started laughing and cackling that she had won. I tackled her, trying to stop her from leaving. We struggled for a moment, but then she struck me with the cooking pan and ran out the back..."

Trussi was instantly filled with anger and grief. He was right! It was the queen in disguise!!

He leaped up, running to the back door. "Baccio, you take care of your wife. I'm going to stop her once and for all!!"

He dashed outside and could see a small figure fleeing toward the woods in the distance. Trussi took several steps forward but realized he had no weapons with him. Quickly glancing around, he saw his pickaxe still lying where he had left it. He grabbed it and took off, running towards the disappearing figure.

Trussi didn't have a plan. He just knew he had to stop her. Tears of anguish formed and flowed down his cheeks freely as he continued running. He had failed to save Snow White. He had failed her! Stopping briefly where he last saw the figure, Trussi could see footprints and followed them. It didn't take him long to realize the direction the steps were heading was toward the apple trees. Even more, anger boiled inside him. He continued running. He just had to stop her. It wasn't long before he was nearly there.

Unexpectedly and suddenly, before him stood Strega, his footsteps stopped quickly, and he nearly ran into her. She was sobbing and reached out, grabbing Trussi's arm and pickaxe.

"Don't go! Please don't go. She'll kill you!!" She begged him desperately. Trussi tried to shrug her off, but her grip only tightened.

"She killed Snow White! If I don't stop her now, how many more have to die because of her jealousy?" He shouted out, frustrated.

Strega sobbed even more deeply. She pulled him into a tight embrace he couldn't escape. "You are right," she cried sadly.

After a moment, she finally released him. "If you truly must go, I have one last gift for you."

Trussi was unsure of what she meant but had him close his eyes. She wiped away some of her tears and reached to Trussi's face, gently touching his closed eyes with her wet fingertips.

"This will protect you from her enchantment. She can no longer keep you motionless."

When he opened his eyes again, she appeared even older and frailer than before.

"Only someone from her bloodline can defeat her. This is why she wants you dead. You are the last one who poses any real threat to her. You may defeat her if you stay strong and use your wits." Her body started to fade, and she fell to the ground. Trussi tried to reach out, but his hand went through her as if nothing was there. She smiled at him.

"That is everything I have to give. Please, Trussi, you must defeat her once and for all. End her terrible reign." Pausing one last time, Strega smiled and said, "You look so much like Vecchia." She closed her eyes and then faded entirely away. Small glowing purple and white flowers were now blooming in the place where she had lain.

Trussi wanted to cry for her, to thank her for all she had done for him. But there was no time. He stood up with even more resolve to stop the queen. Walking forward swiftly, he reached the apple trees. All was quiet, and everything appeared serene. Stepping forward slowly, he looked around.

Again, he felt the hair on the back of his neck stand on end. The queen was undoubtedly here. A sudden bolt of bright light appeared, burning his eyes. Trussi dropped the pickaxe as he grabbed for his eyes. He dived and rolled to his side as quickly as possible to avoid an attack. Luckily the pain only lasted a moment.

Opening his eyes, in front of him stood an old beggar woman. Her eyes glowed green, and her body started contorting and twisting as she changed her shape back into the queen. She smiled at him and eyed him as a predator would before they struck.

"You killed her!" Trussi yelled out. He could feel all the anger and frustration boiling out of him. "You killed her, and she didn't have to die!! We were taking her away. Far away! She would have been-"

Cutting him off, she shouted angrily, "She would have been alive! She could return anytime she chose to!" Her words carried anger and hatred. Her lips then turned into a sneer.

"No. Snow White had to die, Trussi." Her words were now monotone and sounded apathetic.

Trussi could no longer see any beauty about her. She had no empathy, no compassion, and no mercy. Any physical beauty she had was false. It was an illusion made by dark magic. All he could see was how ugly and monstrous she indeed was.

Realizing his pickaxe was close by, he turned and dove for his pickaxe. The queen jetted forward, grabbing his arm as he clasped its handle. It burned where she held him, causing him to drop it again. He fell to his knees, shouting as pain radiated down his arm and into his back.

Her lips curled into a sinister smile as she thrust her head back, letting out a wicked laugh. "Did you think you could vanquish me so easily?!" Trussi pulled but could not get loose from her grip.

"It will take much more than a mere pickaxe to defeat me."

He swiped his leg at her, a feeble attempt at a kick. His leg only met air, and the pain intensified down his arm, causing him to cry out painfully. Trussi tried to reach for the pickaxe, but it was barely close enough that only his fingertips brushed up against it.

Trussi could see the queen pulling out a dagger and raising it above her head. It glittered and glowed green like her eyes, and he could feel the magic surging within it. 'Enchanted with dark magic!!' he frantically thought.

His mind scrambled on what he could do. He had no other weapons, nothing! Looking over at her hand, grasping his arm, he only thought of one thing to do. Surging forward, he bit her hand as hard as possible, drawing dark blood that gushed into his mouth and down the side of his face.

She screamed in surprised pain, dropping her dagger and releasing his arm. The taste in Trussi's mouth was horrendous and smelled of rotten, decayed meat. He didn't hesitate to spit out her blood and quickly reached down to recover his pickaxe. He swung it at her instantly, but the pickaxe missed its mark as the queen had already stumbled back several steps.

"You grisly, horrid little man! How dare you mar my perfect skin!!" Her voice shrieked as she spat out the words.

Seeing her dagger on the ground, she shot forward, reaching to grab it. Trussi swung his pickaxe at her once again. As she held the blade again, she turned suddenly, reaching up and catching the pickaxe's tip in mid-swing.

"Ha! You think you can..." Her voice cut off suddenly. She was shocked as she looked horrified at her hand. Her entire hand had begun turning into sparkling jewels. "This ... is ... not possible!" she shouted as the gems started to form quickly up her forearm.

Trussi quickly pulled his pickaxe out of her jeweled grip and swung it again with all his force. She sidestepped his swing and lifted her leg, kicking him in the chest. Trussi heard a horrible crunching sound as he was quickly thrust backward. He fell on his back, unable to move for a moment. His breath had been knocked out of him, and pain radiated from the impact.

Tears formed in his eyes as his breath finally returned to his desperate lungs. Luckily, he still held his pickaxe and scrambled to stand up, wheezing painfully with every gasp. He could see the queen still held her blade and was already approaching. The jewels had stopped spreading up her arm, but he noticed her hand and forearm had not returned to normal. 'Hope,' he thought.

Her eyes suddenly glowed intensely green, and he could feel every hair on his body stand on end. But her eyes no longer held him, and he could feel his freedom. Standing still, he remained motionless as if her magic still restricted him. He needed her to get close for this to work.

The queen twisted her lips into a crooked smile just then. "Oh, Trussi.... I'm going to make you suffer for what you've done." She licked her lips as she got closer.

This had to work. She just needed to come a little bit closer...

The queen lifted her dagger slightly, pointing it to his chin, and smiled evilly. "I think I'll start here, then end there." She then pointed her blade just below his stomach. She took another step towards him.

Trussi suddenly leaped forward, driving his pickaxe hard into her leg. She turned to avoid the blow but was too close to avoid it altogether. His pickaxe tore through her dress, scraping along the side of her upper leg and calf. Jewels formed everywhere it touched.

The queen shrieked, dropping her dagger once again. Trussi lifted his pickaxe again. Seeing this, she turned to run, but Trussi was now quicker than her. Without hesitation, he struck her firm, square in the back. Screaming, she fell over as her body started convulsing. Jewels formed and spread from where he had made contact. The queen twisted and turned in a feeble attempt to stop what was happening to her.

"You vile, horrid, little..."

Her words were cut off as her face transformed into jewels. She stopped moving, and there, before Trussi, was now a motionless jeweled figure of the queen. Lifting his pickaxe one last time, a look of unbelievable anger on his face, he brought it down hard, completely shattering the figure. All that was left of the queen was now a loose splatter of gemstones.

Trussi fell to his knees. It was over. It was finally over. Looking down at his arm, he saw burn marks where the queen had grabbed him. He needed to head back to Baccio's home and have Doc tend to it.

Thinking this reminded him again of Snow White. The others would have discovered her by now. Tears formed as he thought about how he had failed her. He had defeated queen Regina, but this did nothing to comfort him. Letting go of the pickaxe, Trussi wept. He had lost Giada, Strega, and Snow White. He let all his pain fall out of him, not holding back a single tear.

Finally, after he finished weeping, Trussi lifted himself and started the walk home, leaving everything on the ground behind him. His walk was bleak, and he felt immeasurably exhausted. Each step was punishing and grinding work. Every action, every breath, was painful and tiring. It took everything he had to keep going.

Not even knowing how far he had gone, all of a sudden, he was surrounded by the other dwarves. They had come to help him! He could see they were all asking questions, but his exhaustion prevented him from hearing them. Relief at seeing everyone flooded through him, and Trussi collapsed to the ground. Darkness took over, and he felt no more pain.

****

Slowly waking up, Trussi could hear the bustling of the other dwarves in the distance. He was still so tired. Even though he was waking, it felt like he hadn't slept in a week. Looking around, he could see he was in Baccio's house. He could see Doc asleep in a chair next to him. Groaning with soreness, he slowly sat up. Trussi could see his injured arm was bandaged neatly.

Doc woke up just then and jumped up, startled. "Trussi! You're awake! Thank goodness."

"How long was I out for?" he asked, confused. His voice sounded strained and weak.

Doc looked at him with concerned eyes. "You were out for nearly three days. You had a fever the first two days, and we weren't sure you would make it."

Trussi raised his eyebrows. Was he asleep for three days?

Doc suddenly called out to the others that Trussi was awake. The room was then filled with the rest of his friends, all coming to check in on him. Some patted him on the back, while others expressed relief that he was finally awake. With the room filled with the bustling of dwarves, Baccio's wife pushed through as she carried a large bowl of stew.

"He hasn't eaten in three days! All of you leave him be so he can start eating and regain strength!" Handing Trussi the bowl, she ushered everyone but Doc out of the room.

Trussi ate the stew heartily. His entire body was sore, and he was glad to get something in his stomach. Once finished, Doc checked him over and changed the bandages on his arm. Trussi could see the burn marks were deep but already starting to heal. His chest, however, still hurt tremendously, and Doc informed him he had multiple broken ribs.

Once Doc was done fussing over him, Trussi stood up slowly and walked out of the room, joining the others. Everyone wanted to know what had happened between him and the queen. Deciding they all needed complete truth, he told them what had happened. He told them how Strega had enchanted his pickaxe and how she had helped him just before he fought with the queen. He didn't leave out any detail.

Over the next few days, Trussi rested while preparations for Snow White's funeral went underway. Everyone found it odd, even in death, how very lovely she remained. Her skin did not turn gray, and her cheeks remained rosy as if she were still alive.

Trussi tried to help as much as he could. Although he was improving, he remained frail. Everyone helped build and decorate an elaborate and ornate casket for Snow White. They were adorning it with gold and jewels they had brought with them. Finally, it was befitting their princess.

Lastly, on the day of the burial, they surrounded Snow White with the loveliest flowers they could find. Trussi's heart broke every time he looked at her. 'If only I had come home sooner.' he thought grievously.

Before lowering her casket, each one walked up to Snow White and said something they would miss about her, such as how she sang or was so kind. Trussi went up last, taking his time to speak slowly. He would genuinely miss how wonderful she was to those around her, especially him. Though what he would miss the most were their discussions and how peaceful it was to be around her.

Taking one last deep breath, he leaned in close, whispering, "I will miss you with every part of my heart." Trussi realized there were few in this world he had come to care for. She was one of them. He would more than miss her, and his heart ached to say these words.

"I..." He paused as tears flooded his eyes. "I love you."

Trussi placed a single soft kiss on her cheek. The moment he did, he could instantly see her chest rising and falling. She was breathing! Trussi stood there in shock, unsure if he was dreaming. Everyone gasped as she began to move and stretch her arms.

Sitting up with a yawn, she looked around. "Oh, I'm so sorry! I must have fallen asleep."

Everyone crowded around her, excited at her sudden revival.

Trussi could even see several pinching themselves as they checked to see if they were dreaming. She stood up, yawning again as if she had only been napping. Everyone quickly rushed her, embracing her in hugs and joyous exclamations.

That night, they celebrated Snow White's awakening. Everyone was filled with joy and happiness. Trussi told his story again of how he defeated queen Regina, and every one, along with Snow White, listened attentively. Afterward, they celebrated more with a feast, playing music, and dancing. Trussi found he didn't have the strength to dance but enjoyed clapping along with everyone else. He laughed along, genuinely enjoying the moment and everyone around him.

Once the celebration was over, they began discussing what they should do next. After all, there was still a pile of jewels, the queen's dagger, and Trussi's enchanted pickaxe to contend with. But that, of course, is another story.

ABOUT THE AUTHOR

Elizabeth Gallegos

Growing up in Oregon, I spent much time outdoors as a child. My siblings and I often used our imaginations, sending us on wild adventures.

I am now a New Mexico resident with my husband and two amazing kids. I am blessed to watch them grow and create new memories and adventures with them. My favorite things to do, besides writing, are creating artwork and swimming. There is truly no limit to what we can create on a blank canvas or a page in a book!

To Mike:
A writer, swimmer, painter
Elizabeth Gallegos

Made in the USA
Monee, IL
10 March 2023

29320145R00118